LUCIFER

N.L. HOFFMANN

Lucifer

Cover Art: Under Cover Designs
Editing: Kim's Fiction Proofreading & Editing Services
Interior Formatting: EK Formatting

ACKNOWLEDGMENTS

As always, there are far too many people to thank. *Lucifer* is a big release for me, since my readers begged for him.

My betas, because of their dedicated years with me… Without them, I would be lost and would not push myself to publish.

My editor, because she's fabulous… The things she catches often have me wondering what I was thinking at the time. Hail to the Queen of the Red Pen!

My husband, for his support and always questioning whether or not I'm giving myself enough credit.

Finally, the readers… Your continuous support means everything to me. A lot of you have stuck with me since the beginning. For that, I am grateful.

To Amy…

CHAPTER ONE

MAYE

"Well, I really want brownies, but I'm too lazy to get up and make them," I said from my prone position on the couch.

I was so drained, I felt like throwing a tantrum, like a toddler. But even doing that seemed like too much effort. Being this exhausted was ridiculous. Working as much as I did was even more so, but I had to pay bills. Hell, I should be happy I could make a living doing something I loved. Who else could say they sold enough art to pay rent? Not a lot of people…until after they died anyway.

Most of my time was spent in my apartment painting, then giving my art to Parker, who sold it for me in his gallery. I now used a pseudonym, a necessity after my run-in with an obsessive older lady.

Most of my art ideas came from touching people, seeing into their minds. It wasn't your usual psychic ability. I couldn't glimpse the future, but I could see what they'd done during their lifetime…good and bad. It was almost as if I could see into their soul. Some would think having an ability like that would be amazing, but it wasn't. When I connected with somebody, I felt like I was in that time and place, no matter how long ago it happened.

"I can go get something from the diner," Parker offered. "I'll even pay for it because this painting is going to make us both a lot of money. I'm not even joking about that." He put a hand to his chin and cupped his elbow as he stared at it. "Oh yeah. This is going to be your most expensive piece yet. I wish I knew how you came up with this stuff. Some are dark and creepy. Then you have the ones that remind me of angels. Those are my favorite. Does it have to do with whether or not you're on your period?"

Not wanting to have this conversation, I rolled from the couch and onto the floor, crawling to my shoes. "That's gross, and no, I don't want anything from the diner. I want dessert. You're too slow anyway."

He turned and watched me. "And crawling is faster?" He chuckled, running a hand through his blond curls. He was gorgeous. Perfect body, perfect teeth, perfect hair, beautiful blue eyes, expensive suit. It was too bad he wasn't into ladies.

Laughing, I fell flat onto the floor. "I'm just so tired. But I need to get out and get some inspiration," I said, reaching out for my shoes and putting them on with a groan, then falling back onto the floor. Maybe I could convince Parker to tie them for me.

"I don't like what happens to you when you touch someone, Maye." His jovial expression fell. "It's strange. The person you touch has no idea it's even happening. I've never seen anything like it before. It's like watching a horror movie."

I sighed. Parker only saw it happen one time not too long ago, but once I explained it was normal for me, he wouldn't quit bringing it up. He continuously asked questions, and I would explain more of it each time, but I wasn't in the mood now. I was exhausted, ready to punch someone in the face for one wrong word.

"I will tell you all about it one day, Parker. But right now, I'm just too tired."

"We're best friends. I should have known about this two years ago, Maye. How is it I am just now finding out about it? You've touched me so many times. How come it never happened with you and me?"

There it was. He wanted to know if I saw anything when I touched him. I sat up and groaned. "Can't this wait?"

Parker hurried over and sat on the floor. "Oh no, girlfriend. I have you trapped. Time to open up to your BFF."

I sighed. "What I see with you is a pure heart. You always go out of your way for people, for both those you love and those you don't. You have a problem with being the bad guy, even when the person's a dick. The one thing that stands out the most is the unrequited love you have for someone you've known for years." I cocked my head at him. "You really should find that person and tell him how you feel. It will complete your soul."

Parker stared at me, eyes wide.

I slowly climbed to my feet. "Now, I'm ready to get my damn dessert. No more questions, got it?"

I glanced over at the TV, seeing a news story about the latest murder in the city. The second one in as many weeks. They warned everyone to not go out alone. Maybe going for dessert was a bad idea.

"Hello? Earth to Maye?"

I turned to Parker and raised my eyebrows. What was he doing on the floor wearing his expensive suit? I looked down at my ripped jeans, the t-shirt with a cartoon cupcake on it. I didn't really care what I wore. I had no one to impress. Sometimes Parker bought me clothes, then they sat in my closet until he forced me to go out. He always said something about *getting fresh air* and *being social.* I liked being a hermit. People pissed me off.

A few minutes later, we walked downstairs and headed down the street. The diner was just a block away. The cool, fall air woke me enough that there wasn't much complaining on my part. Parker shook his head at my newfound enthusiasm. We would probably have to hail a taxi to get back home since a warm brownie topped with ice cream would probably make me sleepy.

It was still early enough that most shops lining the street were still open. I looked into my favorite one, which contained antiques and other items you couldn't always find in other stores. I was just about to walk past when I spotted an older easel sitting in the back.

I snagged Parker's arm and pointed. "We need to go in and look at that."

"The place is closing for the day." Parker said, inclining his head to the man inside, who just flipped the sign over to closed.

Gasping, I hurried over to the glass door. I tapped on it, motioning for the older man to come back to the door. When he opened it a crack, I smiled. "Can I please come in? I need to see that easel in the back before someone else buys it."

The man seemed to think about it, rubbing his white beard as he contemplated. Finally, he smiled, nodding and opening the door wider. "Good thing you caught me. I would have ignored most people, but I'm in a good mood." He motioned us to follow. "A few people have looked at this, so if you want it, you probably should buy it now…and I'm not saying that because I want a sale." He winked at me, then yawned loudly before walking back behind the counter. "I have to start closing down, so let me know when you're ready."

I didn't say anything, too focused on the easel in front of me. It was old and looked as if it would buckle under the weight of a canvas. There was a drawer at the center, but when I tugged on it, it didn't budge.

Parker sighed. "This is a piece of shit, Maye. I can buy you a better one. Something that doesn't look like it might collapse on you. We don't want any of that awesome art ruined, do we?"

I glared at him. "It's sturdy. I need this." I flipped the tag over and gasped at the price. "But not for that amount." I worried my bottom lip, thinking about having to talk the guy down, but before I could move, Parker grabbed a large wooden box sitting next to it, then dragged the easel closer to the register.

Parker called out, "Old man, we'll take these items."

The guy chuckled when he came out of the back room. "Okay, but the cat comes with it."

"What?" both Parker and I said at the same time, not sure what he was talking about.

"When I got the easel in the shop, the cat came with it. And she won't leave." He frowned down at a spotted cat that walked out from behind the counter. She meowed, then looked up at me with intelligent eyes. Something seemed off about her, but when I bent down to stroke her soft fur, I smiled. Maybe I could use a roommate.

I sighed, debating. Something niggled at the back of my mind, but when Parker opened his mouth to object, I nodded.

"Fine. We'll take the cat, too."

CHAPTER TWO
LUCIFER

"Dear gods, what's with the rocking around?"

I held my arms out to try and steady myself.

All I had was the damn lantern Aden had left me, nothing else. I looked around the small area. Reminding me of the worst parts of Hell, it smelled like wood and something I couldn't put a finger on. I heard wind whistling from somewhere.

This was my punishment for streaking at the football game? That was normal behavior for me! Was it the gift of speedos? He knew speedos were my favorite. I couldn't even imagine what I did to piss him off. He was awfully sensitive lately. Nothing I did required such a harsh punishment.

"Come out, Aden! I know you're watching me, you damn pervert. You have yet to explain why I'm here," I yelled.

"No shouting, brother. You may be heard, and we can't have that before the time is right."

Aden appeared, glowing in all his glory. Whenever he appeared and disappeared, it was just for show. The only thing missing was dramatic music. I averted my burning eyes, almost regretting looking directly at him. They say you weren't supposed to set your gaze on him. My eyes felt like they were about to burst into flames, but by blinking through the tears, I managed to get through it. *Bastard*. He was lucky I didn't wear my speedos and give him quite the show. It could blind a person for eternity.

Once his light died down, I crossed my arms over my chest, frowning at him. "Why have you brought me here? I thought we agreed five hundred years ago that this wouldn't happen anymore? Did you lie? You know you cannot lie."

Aden looked away, trying to hide a smile. His white suit was impeccable, as usual, blond hair neatly brushed back, as if slathered in gel. Someone should seriously give him lessons on proper hair maintenance.

"Come now, brother," I said, gesturing for him to speak. "Let's not have any secrets between us. I would like to get out of this place as soon as possible."

"Remember five hundred years ago when you agreed to do a few good deeds? Well, it's time. Time to make up for all the evil you've done in the world." Aden placed his hands on his hips, pushing back his suit coat from his toned body.

I frowned. "I thought helping the girls take down Nick was enough good for at least a hundred years."

At the mention of that name, Aden sighed. Our brother had wanted to live in the normal world for a while, but eventually, he turned very dark. People died, and the world was close to ending due to his destruction. With the aid of my daughters, we managed to defeat him. Despite the things he did, we still missed him.

"Yeah, well, we have much more to do, Lucifer. The world is at risk once again."

"Use your godly powers to fix it!" I snapped, agitated.

I could laugh at a good joke like anybody else, but this was my freedom we were talking about. I had havoc to create, people to convince that being bad was the only way to go. I had my devil duties! The King of Hell never took a vacation. If this could even be called one! Didn't Aden have minions to help him?

Rage started building, and I felt my horns starting to elongate. Aden glanced at the top of my head, then took a menacing step toward me.

"You won't help me with this?" he demanded.

I sighed, looking away. He was trying to make me feel bad. Too bad no one could make me care. "Will you wear the speedos I gave you for your birthday?" I asked, cocking my head at him.

Frowning, Aden turned away to look into the darkness of the room. "I guess I will agree, but you must finish this! This woman needs your help. I can't have you sidetracked. You have the attention span of a toddler."

I raised my eyebrows, ignoring his last sentence. "Woman? Is it someone famous? I always did want to do bad things with that one actress." I smirked. "You know, the one in that one movie?"

Aden was suddenly inches from my face. "You will *not* sleep with this one," he growled.

I crossed my arms. "Or what?"

I winced, my pants seeming to tighten. When I pulled back the waistband and looked inside, I growled in anger. "Are you fucking kidding me? You can't put a damn chastity belt on me, Aden. The devil will not be told no. Take it off." I snapped my fingers.

Shaking his head, Aden began to glow. "No can do, brother. Looks like you have to keep it in your pants."

"I *will not* keep it in my pants!" I shouted as he disappeared, his quiet laughter echoing.

CHAPTER THREE

We stared at my new easel sitting by the window. The moon shone through the glass, casting a glow over it. It was beautiful. Parker probably saw a piece of crap, but I saw something special. When I had tried to open the drawer again, it remained closed. I knew something was in there because when we carried it up the steps to the apartment, I heard something rattling.

Sighing in contentment, I kissed Parker on the cheek. "Thank you for buying this. The price was a little too steep for me."

"Yeah, I kind of figured that when you dropped the price tag like it burned your fingers. You should really stop being stingy with your money. I know you're used to not having much, but you have enough now to spend a little every once in a while. When I present your newest piece, I have a feeling you'll be able to pay your rent for over a year."

Smiling, I walked over to the box on my dining table and played with the metal lock. "Why did you buy this?"

He shrugged. "Looked like it went with the easel." He came over to stand next to me, his cologne filling my nostrils, a comforting shiver washing over me. He was my rock. Without him, I would be alone and afraid. Probably would never go outside.

I lifted the box, finding a key taped to the bottom. When I ripped it off, some of the old wood came with it. I winced, wishing I'd been more careful. I stuck the key into the lock and turned.

The lid fought me for a few brief moments, but it finally opened with a creak, revealing an old, leather-bound book. I glanced over at Parker, who shrugged. He was right about it looking like it went with the easel, due to the wood appearing similar, but the book didn't make any sense. When I ran my finger over the metal lock securing it, it popped open. Weird… Maybe it was broken.

Biting my lower lip, I took the book out and started to open it, but an odd feeling crept over my skin. It reminded me of bugs, thousands of tiny legs crawling over my skin. I jumped back in alarm, tossing the book onto the table.

"What the fuck?" I shivered, unable to shake the feeling.

"What happened?" Parker asked, alarmed. He grabbed my hands, turning them over to look at them. When he found nothing, his confused gaze met mine. "Are you high? Your pupils are huge. Is it meth? You didn't take any candy from anyone, did you?"

I shook out my hands and slowly walked back over to the book. "Touch it."

Parker furrowed his brows, then pressed his hands to the dark leather. "Okay…"

"You don't feel anything?"

Shaking his head, he lifted the book. "Nope. You're being a crazy bitch, Maye. Calm down and breathe."

"Try opening it."

"Okay, sister." He flipped open the book. "Nothing. Just blank pages." That seemed strange. Parker set the book back down. "You're fine. I'm fine. Everyone is fine. Touch it again."

"Why are the pages blank?" I reached for the book, then stopped. "No." I grabbed the broom next to me and used it to push the book away. "I might look at it later, but for now, that shit can stay over there."

He shrugged, glancing down at his watch. "Listen, I have to go. I told Becca I would close the gallery tonight since she has to go to her brother's birthday party." He yawned. "I may just close early." As I stared at the book, not saying anything, he patted me on the back. "Maybe you should think about a nap before you start your next project."

"That book is weird. Something is off about it, Parker."

"I'll take your word for it, Maye. If anything else happens, give me a call." When I nodded, he smiled. "And get the litter box ready before the cat shits somewhere." He chuckled.

I looked around, remembering the cat. The spotted feline appeared and meowed. Parker and I looked at each other.

"Did she just say 'fuck you'? I mean, it sounded like it," I said, confident the cat actually spoke.

Parker seemed to think about that, then shook his head. "Cats can't talk. Maybe you *are* high." He laughed, snatching up the painted canvas and hurrying out the door before I could stop him.

Shaking my head, I walked to the cat box and poured in some litter. I didn't want a cat, but I did want that damn easel. Something told me I had to have it, so I was willing to take on a pet just so I could get it. I placed her box in the corner of the room and sighed.

A box for pooping. How lovely.

After I set down her food and water, I returned to the easel and placed a blank canvas on it. I smiled, debating what I wanted to paint. Then I knew. *Him.* Whoever he was, I had his image in my mind for a while and knew I had to paint him. It was as if something took over my body. I felt my mind go far away, focusing.

It felt like just minutes had passed, but when I glanced at the clock, I saw it was already five in the morning. I looked at my completed canvas. He was handsome, someone I felt like I already knew. His dark hair was swept back, eyes changed from blue to green, depending on his mood, infectious laugh. He was my safe zone. But who was he?

CHAPTER FOUR
LUCIFER

I didn't know how much longer I could stay here. The lantern didn't seem like it would stay lit much longer. I tried using my powers to get out, unsuccessfully. I could make light and even a drink from Hell, yet I couldn't get out of here? It pissed me off. I called out to Aden many times, to no avail.

Humming, I lay on the floor, placing my hands behind my head. I yawned, debating about a short nap. Something was bound to happen eventually, right? Just as I closed my eyes, the whole room began to shake.

What the bloody hell?

It shook again. I scrambled up and held onto the wall, feeling my stomach roil violently with the movement. *The devil does not throw up.* Closing my eyes briefly, I waited for the movement to stop. When it finally did, I felt a cool breeze, a light shining down on me.

"What the fuck?"

The angelic voice was like music to my ears, though a tad bit loud. I opened my eyes and looked up…seeing a giant! I ran to the other side of the room, frantically looking around.

Dear gods, what has Aden left me to? He is mad if he thinks my size will help this person.

She stared at me, stunned, eyes wide. After what seemed like hours, she finally spoke in a low voice. "Are you a tiny person? I didn't think people could be this small. Is it a new disease? I mean, they discover new things every day," she rambled.

"Love, you're the damn giant. Let me out of here."

She narrowed her eyes. "A bit demanding, aren't you? I don't listen to people who demand things. I like words such as *please* and *thank you*. I bet your momma didn't raise an asshole."

"I don't even know who my mother is. And I don't use those words very often, so you'll have to remind me."

One wary eye on her, I jumped up to grab the top of the box, struggling to find a toehold and pull myself out. This was ridiculous. How was I supposed to help a giant?

Deciding I had enough, I used my powers. Immediately, I was back to normal size and lying on the floor, looking around. When she let out a little shriek, I glanced at her. She wasn't a giant. Then I looked at the contraption she stood by, drawer open.

What the fuck? I was in *there*? Next time I saw him, I'd wring Aden's neck. He would have to let me, of course, which was unlikely.

Standing and brushing off my suit, smoothing my hair by running my hands over it, I glanced at the woman. She was gorgeous. Stunning. I'd never seen anyone with her kind of beauty before. Her lightly tanned skin reminded me of the women in Egypt, though they were a shade or two darker. Her black hair was straight and long, reaching to just above her ass. But the most gorgeous things were her blue eyes. So blue, they reminded me of the oceans in Bali.

I'd seen many women in my lifetime, even ones of their own creation, but their beauty could not compare. She outshone all of them. Though, I had to admit, I could just be horny. I never went a day without getting laid.

That was when I realized the chastity belt was no longer present. The stiff, cold, uncomfortable feeling was now gone. I blew out a breath, relieved. Last thing I needed was to be clanking around. She would ask questions and things would get awkward.

"So, let's get this over with. How can I help you?" I said, straightening my cuffs with impatient, jerky movements. She may be gorgeous, but I wanted to complete this as soon as possible. Getting laid could come later.

Was it wrong of me to think of her this way? Probably. But I'd tried long-term relationships before, with disastrous results. The women usually ended up being controlling and crazy…literally. It could have been my fault, but if someone couldn't accept you the way you were, they weren't *the one*.

She wrapped her arms around herself, as if for protection. "I don't need anything from you. Why were you in my easel? How the hell did you grow bigger? How did you even become small in the first place? I don't get what's happening here."

When I didn't respond, she studied me for a few minutes.

If she didn't need my help, why was I here? Too many questions, not enough answers.

"I was sent here to help you with something," I said slowly, almost as if she didn't understand English. "So, what do you need help with, love?"

The woman seemed to become impatient. She placed her hands on her hips and frowned. "Unless you know how to paint—"

"She doesn't need you for anything, loser," a feminine voice said from another room.

"Who the hell was that?" the female whispered.

I waited for someone to appear. A spotted cat poked her head around the corner and showed me her fangs.

"I have this handled. We don't need *Lucifer* to save the day. Like that's even possible. You're too much of a prick."

The woman gasped. "Did she just talk?"

"What is your name?" I asked the woman, ignoring the cat.

"Maye… Wait, I don't want to talk to you. Get the hell out of my apartment." She pointed to the door.

I shrugged and took a step, then heard Aden whisper that he would lock me up for five hundred years if I didn't do as he needed.

Asshole.

I sighed and turned back to her. "Well, Maye, your cat can talk because she's Cleopatra. Apparently, she was naughty and someone thought she should pay for her sins before crossing over." I looked at the cat and laughed. "Kind of a long time trying to prove yourself."

Cleo sent me a dark look before she sat and began to lick her paw. I was pretty sure she just flipped me off, but I didn't know if cat toes could move that way.

I turned away from her to look at Maye, who just stared at the cat. Then she looked at me, smirking. "She just flipped you off."

I shrugged. "Doesn't surprise me. I bet that adds to the bad kitty behavior, though. Shouldn't you be a good girl and go use the litter box?"

That earned a glare from Cleo, but she walked back into the room she had come out of, mumbling something that probably would have added years to her punishment. Why was she even here? Things didn't add up. Aden obviously left out a lot of vital information. He was good at that. I felt like I had to solve some kind of riddle half the time.

"So, I was in this…art contraption?" I asked, gesturing to it.

She snorted. "It's an easel, and yes, I found you in the drawer. I don't know why you were there, and I don't even care. I just want you gone. My life does not need your kind of complicated." She looked from the easel to me, as if trying to figure everything out. "This is insane!" she growled in frustration, throwing her hands up. "Just get out of here. And take the damn cat with you."

I looked at her with raised eyebrows. "*My* kind of complicated? How am I a complication? I've come to save the day."

"The cat called you Lucifer. If that's true, what can the King of Hell possibly do for me...other than take my soul?" she demanded, seemingly becoming increasingly irritated with my presence. I was not used to this type of dismissive behavior from women. The way she acted confused me.

CHAPTER FIVE

MAYE

"Sometimes I do good things," he whispered, almost as if hurt.

I laughed. I couldn't help it. The man was incredibly handsome, but I couldn't let on that I thought that. His ego would grow even bigger. "I don't care if you have. The devil is bad news. You may start out wanting to help, but in the end, it'll be all about you. I've never heard of Satan doing good things for people. That goes against his very nature."

He threw up his hands. "That's what *I* said! But my brother insists. So, here I am! Ready to get to work, love." He winked at me, which only made me want to smack him. Did he think this stuff actually worked? Okay, it did, but he was getting on my nerves.

As if sensing it, he turned to look at the painting on the easel and smiled broadly. "Oh, that's gorgeous. You caught every good side of me, but I have to admit, I don't have any *bad* side." He nodded his approval, finger on his chin. "Very impressive. I am devilishly handsome." Nudging me with his elbow, he grinned. "Get it? Devilishly?"

I groaned. "Okay, time to go." I started shoving him toward the door of my apartment. "I know this isn't the way you came in, but I think the devil can find his way around the city. Do you need me to call a taxi?" I paused to grab my phone, dialing before he responded.

Suddenly, Lucifer stopped moving toward the door. When I tried to push him again, it was like shoving against a brick wall. "You have something of mine," he growled, facing me, an expression on his face that probably killed many people who saw it. His eyes were red, sinister, completely unnatural.

I stepped back. "What do you mean? I don't have anything of yours. And c-can you change your eyes back? That's creeping me out."

He ignored me as he brushed past. My body started trembling. Was this what the devil was really like? Dangerous, the air crackling around him, threatening violence if no one did what he asked? I felt sorry for his demon minions.

Did he *have* minions? I assumed, but figured he probably had *something* serving him. And why wasn't I freaking out? Something was definitely wrong with me.

Focusing on Lucifer, I watched as he walked toward the book. I rushed over and stood in front of it, blocking it from view. "That's mine." I was suddenly very protective of it, ready to go against the devil. That was insane! But at that moment, I did not want him to have it.

"Ten minutes ago, a woman was found in the Riverfront Park. Police think it's the work of the serial killer who murdered two victims in their homes. We don't know all the details yet, but she was found alive, albeit barely, and is currently being transported to the hospital. More details as we get them. Be alert. It wouldn't surprise this newscaster if a city-wide curfew is soon put into effect."

I wasn't sure why that drew my attention, but I turned to the TV, seeing an ambulance leaving the park. Shaking my head, I turned and raised my eyebrows when Lucifer cleared his throat.

"I will find out why I am here. For now, Maye, you need to stay in your apartment, just in case." He walked toward the door.

I snorted. "Just in case what?" I strode over to the easel and shoved in the drawer. "I have to paint anyway, so I don't plan on leaving for a while."

Hesitating before he placed a hand on the doorknob, Lucifer looked to the room the cat had come out of, seeing her sitting there. "Cleo, keep an eye on her. I *will* talk to you later."

"Whatever, prick."

"Dear gods, the feline has a mouth on her. I can only imagine what she was like as a human." Not saying another word, he left the apartment.

Moving quickly, I locked the door and hoped he would never return. When I looked at my canvas, I wondered how I had painted the perfect likeness.

*

I typically never dreamed, but when I did, it was usually bad, of another time that never existed.

It seemed I was in Hell. The fiery pits called to me, chanting my name. Souls hovered over the fire, screaming as they burned for their sins. I cringed every time. And it wasn't just one time that they went through this. It repeated. I knew they experienced something I could not, but had I been able to touch them as a human, all their secrets would have been revealed.

I screamed myself awake, bolting up in bed. Sunlight streamed through the window, telling me I slept far too late. What did I expect when I went to bed at seven am? After Lucifer's visit, it took me a while to fall asleep. I lay there, listening to Cleo get into things. Even though she had been a human at one time, she sure perfected how to act like a pain in the ass cat. Maybe a spray bottle was needed in order to show her I was boss in my own apartment.

I rolled onto my side. According to the alarm clock, it was only ten in the morning. I felt dead, my body heavy. This was worse than yesterday. What the fuck was going on? Should I be this exhausted?

Hearing the buzzer for my door, I moaned, climbed out of bed, and went to answer the intercom. "Hello?" No one answered, which was odd. Then again, it was probably kids playing a prank.

Yawning, I walked into the kitchen to make myself something to eat. I was starving. We never did get my brownie and ice cream. I made a mental note to do that tonight.

Again, the buzzer sounded. Getting annoyed, I strode over to it and pushed the button. "Get away from my door, you little assholes!"

"Excuse me?" a man asked.

I froze, not sure what to say. Finally, I cleared my throat and leaned against the wall. "Sorry. I thought you were kids playing a prank."

"Calling children assholes is hardly adult behavior," came the aggravated reply.

Shaking my head, I debated even unlocking the door and allowing whomever it was in. The man sounded older and unfamiliar. "Who are you?" I asked, not ready to press that open button.

"I'm here for the book. You need to get rid of it before someone comes for you."

I started to respond when the hairs on the back of my neck stood on end. I slowly turned around, startling when I saw Lucifer standing by the box. Somehow the book managed to get back into it.

"I wouldn't let him up if I were you. Do you know how many people are after this book?" When I didn't respond, he sighed, his fingertips barely touching the box. "This is mine. The only reason I haven't taken it back is because there's obviously a reason it's here. It wouldn't just disappear. I think someone stole it, but it knows to escape when possible. Whoever took it didn't put the proper safeguards in place. You need spells and other sorts of magic barriers to keep it guarded. That's why it's in this box."

The buzzer sounded again. When I reached for the button, Lucifer was suddenly next to me, grabbing my wrist.

"I wouldn't. Whoever that is wants the book."

"That's what he said. He's being honest so far."

"This book shouldn't be in anyone else's hands but mine."

He released my wrist, leaving a warm sensation behind. I wanted him to touch me again, but knew asking would make me sound like a freak, not to mention inflate his ego. Was what he said true? And why the fuck did I still talk to him like him being here wasn't insane? I had major problems if I was willing to accept so much without asking questions. Anyone else would have run away screaming.

"How did you get in here?" I asked, looking around. I only had one door.

Lucifer laid a hand on the box. "I can come and go as I please. Luckily, Aden needs me to help you, so he hasn't put many restrictions on me. Though he seems to think it's damn funny that I was in the easel. We should destroy it. No one uses those things anymore anyway."

He started walking toward it, but I ran in front of him, holding my arms out to my sides.

"No! It's mine!" I glared at him, daring him to try and get around me. Maybe he would touch me again...

Shit, what the hell was wrong with me? I didn't care about men. Thus far, the only experience I'd had turned out to be jerks or had an agenda, so I stayed away from them as much as possible...other than Parker.

He stopped and stared at me, as if wanting to say something, then looked away, leaving me cold. I didn't understand my attraction to him. He was the King of Hell, and I was obviously drawn to evil. That didn't say much for me. I should probably start going to church before I sealed my fate to the fiery pits. Maybe Lucifer would rescue me and we would live happily ever after.

Not. Quit being so delusional, Maye.

"Have you tried to read the book yet?" he asked, opening the box.

Running toward it, I shoved him away. "That's mine, too."

"What?! I think not! I made this book with my souls! You can't have it." He grabbed my arms, pinning them to my sides, lifted, and moved me over about a foot. "Now, if you'll excuse me…" He reached into the box and pulled out the book, examining it with a strange, faraway look in his eyes. "Yes," he breathed. "It would be catastrophic if this fell into the wrong hands."

"I don't understand."

When he started to open it, I took a step back. He furrowed his brows. "What's wrong?"

"The book makes me feel…weird."

He shook his head and opened it. "To anyone else who tried to read it, the pages would look blank. I'm the only one who can see what this book contains." He smiled, obviously pleased with that fact.

"Oh, I can read it," I said, stepping back some more. "It just creeps me out, so you need to close it and put it back into the box." I shivered, having the overwhelming urge to run away. It was a strange feeling. I could sense the book calling me, asking me to touch it. The sensation was almost addictive, and I had only touched it one time. Maybe giving it to someone else was a good idea.

Lucifer scowled and opened his mouth, but I turned toward the door when the buzzer sounded again. I glanced at Lucifer with a questioning gaze. He shrugged and closed the book, put it back into the box, then walked to the buzzer.

"We don't want any."

"Lucifer," the person hissed. "How did you get to the book before we did?"

"My powers, of course. Get the hell out of here before I set your soul on fire. This book doesn't belong to you. Do you really want to get on my bad side, Rico?"

I heard him gasp.

"You know who I am?" he asked in surprise.

"I recognize *all* my minions, and now that I know you have turned on me, you *will* suffer the consequences. I'll give you a ten-minute head start. One… Two…" Lucifer sighed and turned to me. "Can never trust a demon, you know."

"That's exactly how I feel, so if you don't mind…" I gestured to the door. "I'm sure there is someone else's soul you can steal." I crossed my arms over my chest.

He frowned, as if insulted. "I do not *steal souls*."

I didn't know it was possible to insult the devil.

CHAPTER SIX
LUCIFER

Did she just say I stole souls? Did my charm not persuade her of my convincing ways? Feeling as if I'd met my match, I grinned.

"Challenge accepted."

She shook her head slightly, frowning. "Wait… What?"

I smirked. As long as I understood she was now a shiny new toy for me to play with, I would get her to like me in no time. I looked over at the box, debating about just disappearing with it.

When I had left before, I tried to find Aden, but the asshole disappeared. Finally, after I screamed that I would run through a nearby shopping mall naked if he didn't show himself, he agreed to meet with us, saying there was much for Maye to know. Whatever that meant. Aden had always been full of secrets…usually ones that ended badly for me.

Pounding on the apartment door had us both turning our heads. Apparently, even after I threatened him, the minion was not going to give up. I sighed and motioned Maye to get into the other room as I gathered my power. Then I waited patiently as the demon banged on and kicked her door.

I studied my nails, barely flinching when the door burst open. I smiled at Rico. Behind him stood three more…Ashley, Esther, and Bianca. I nodded, impressed. He'd decided to bring some of the strongest of all my demons. Unfortunately, they weren't the brightest, which was why they agreed to work with the idiot in the first place.

I rubbed my nails lightly on my suit coat. "Well, look at this little reunion." I shook my head, tsking. "You left Hell without permission. I'll notify Alexa of your return."

They all attacked, shooting balls of electricity, as if it would phase me. I was quicker than any of my demons. Yet when one of the glowing balls managed to hit me, I vibrated with intense agony. I clenched my teeth as the pain worked its way through my body.

"We got a bit more power than you remember," Rico chuckled, throwing another ball of energy.

The three women advanced, each throwing out their power. I leapt out of the way of each one, avoiding exploding furniture as I did. Dear gods, they were serious about trying to take me down. I wasn't going to allow that to happen.

I decided enough was enough. Had we been outside, I would have messed with them some more. But I didn't want them to completely destroy Maye's apartment.

"How about some good, old-fashioned fighting?" I asked.

I struck out, hitting Rico twice in the face. He groaned as bone crunched, falling to the floor. I kicked Ashley in the face, then spun to kick Bianca in the ribs. The ladies went down easier than I expected. They were strong, but they weren't focused enough to actually hit me with much power. When they did, I could work through the pain without hesitating. I'd probably be sore later, though.

Knowing fighting was futile, Esther ran toward the door. I rolled my own power between my hands. It was black, smoky, and had blue lightning bolts weaving through it. I threw it like a baseball, pleased when it hit her and she screamed, falling onto the floor, a smoldering hole in her back. I cringed. It looked painful, but she had already passed out. Even demons had a pain threshold.

Turning to Rico writhing the floor, holding his face, I grasped his collar and lifted him, holding his bleeding face close to mine. "You thought you could take me?"

Rico sputtered blood. "The book is missing, and everyone is trying to find it. With it, anyone can take over your seat, be in control."

"How do you figure?" I demanded, feeling my anger rise at the fact my demons dared to go against me. Hell I was the strongest, yet they thought if they banded together, they could take me down? I wanted to laugh, but I didn't. I remained focused on Rico, waiting.

"There is a bounty on your head, boss. Whoever kills you and brings back the book gets the throne."

"Why not just kill me and forget about the book?" I asked through clenched teeth.

Rico coughed, his eyes rolling to the back of his head. Had he fought a human, he wouldn't be hurt, but considering my power far exceeded his, the injuries were severe. Annoyed, I pressed my hand to his forehead, instructing Alexa to make sure he suffered. His body burst into flames, disappearing.

I went to do the same with the others, ignoring Maye standing in the doorway of the room, eyes wide. She gasped when the bodies burst into flames and disappeared.

"What the hell are you doing to these people?" she demanded. She grabbed my arm before I could walk to Esther.

Straightening, I pried her hand off mine. "They aren't human."

"Still. Werewolves, vampires, whatever… They don't deserve this."

I shrugged, bending down. "Demons. And they *do* deserve it. There's a reason they were sent to me in the first place." Esther burst into flames and disappeared.

Maye placed her hands on her hips. "I'll stop you if you try to do it again."

I laughed loudly. "I'd like to see you try." At her scowl, I cocked my head. "Dear gods, you're cute."

She gaped. "What the fuck? I am not *cute*!" She shoved me, surprising me with her strength. My breastbone actually felt tender, but I didn't let her know that. I'd ask Aden about it later.

"Listen, we have a lot to do. Everyone obviously knows you have the book, and *apparently*, someone is out to dethrone me, so we need to move. I can't go back to Hell, so it looks like we have to find another place to stay." I sighed heavily, trying to figure out where to go. There were probably some vacant houses around.

She raised her eyebrows. "Notice how you say someone is out to dethrone *you*? Well, it sounds like I am not involved in any way, so the safest thing for me would be for you to leave."

"You don't understand what's happening here. The book you have is currently wanted by every supernatural being out there. Demons will come for me, but you have the book. Let me take it, and maybe you can avoid all of this mess."

She shook her head, looking over at the box. "I can't give it up. It's mine."

"No, it's mine."

"Not anymore." She walked over to the box, pulled the book out, and held it to her chest. "This book came to me for a reason, so it belongs to me."

I reached for it, but the book jumped out of her arms and landed onto the table, causing Maye to let out a small shriek. I stared at it in confusion. "I know you think you know what's best, but I need to take you back to Hell." Most people would think it ridiculous to talk to a book, but this one was very much alive. I grabbed for it again, but it jumped off the table and to the floor.

"What the hell is it doing?" Maye whispered, baffled.

I sighed, placing my hands on my hips. "Well, it apparently wants to stay with you. I'm not sure exactly why. I mean, you're definitely hot, but not to the point where I would want to live with you twenty-four/seven. I'd probably blow my head off after a day or two." When she didn't reply, I glanced over to see her furrowed brow. "Anyway, this book is alive. It's made from souls and very much has its own personality."

"You would blow your head off?" She sounded a little hurt.

"*That's* what you focused on? I just explained to you the book is made from souls, yet you're upset about that part of the conversation?" I shook my head in disbelief, then whistled at the book. It shuffled a few inches away.

"If you can't stand to be around me, I'm definitely not going with you. I'll stay right here." She tossed back her long, black hair, blue eyes blazing with anger.

Why was she so upset? It didn't make any sense when she obviously didn't like me in the first place. I knew I was being an ass. That came naturally, and there was usually no stopping what came out of my mouth. Had she been somebody else, I would flirt with her more. But since she seemed to be Aden's project, I had to be somewhat polite. As polite as the devil could be anyway.

"Ah, dear Maye, we have no choice but to stay together. I will arrange a new place for us. My daughter, Blake, has many safe houses."

I pulled out my cell phone and scrolled for her number. I could just pop over to her home, but last time I did that, she and Eli were in the middle of a...situation, so I had to leave suddenly. Since then, she had threatened to harm me if I just showed up. I wasn't in the mood to deal with the little pain in the ass.

Maye snatched my phone from me.

"Hey, I just purchased that," I said.

She held it up. "Since when does the devil use a cell phone?"

"Since they were invented." I rolled my eyes. "Dear gods, woman. I am not a hermit. I enjoy technology as much as the next person. I may be as old as the world, but I do keep up with the times."

I grabbed my phone back from her and pressed it to my ear. When Blake answered, I smiled. "Hello, darling daughter. I need a favor."

CHAPTER SEVEN

MAYE

Looking into the closet, I frowned. Why were there so many speedos in a damn safe house? Who willingly wore these things?

Seeing something out of the corner of my eye, I looked into the hall, frowning. A man's ass in freaking speedos! I let my eyes roam up his toned back, taking time to admire the tattoos I'd never seen the likes of before. I was mostly baffled about the speedos, though. He dug around in the linen closet, obviously looking for something. When he pulled out a kitchen towel, I decided to see what he was up to.

"Lucifer?" I asked.

"Yes, love?" He turned his head. "Well, look at you. Are you settling in? Did you see the swimsuit I had Blake bring you?"

"Are you talking about the one with the glowing nipples?" He nodded with a smile. "Thanks, but I'll pass." I shook my head in disbelief. He had to have chosen that. Why his daughter would make sure it was in the house was beyond me.

He frowned. "Why? It matches my speedos." He gestured toward his junk, which glowed with red lights.

"Uh, okay." I closed the bedroom door so I could be alone.

I looked at the canvases I brought along. I had covered up the one of him, disturbed and stunned I had painted it before even setting eyes on him. Being around him made my heart pound erratically. I wasn't sure whether it was because I liked him or if the situation was starting to get to me. Maybe I didn't even want to know.

He does have a nice ass…

I looked around the room. The furniture was cheap, the comforter and pillowcases a plain red color. Nothing fancy. The blinds on the windows were drawn. When I tried to pull the string to raise them, they wouldn't move.

"Trying to see outside?"

I jumped and spun, seeing Lucifer standing in the doorway, chuckling, Cleo walking up behind him.

"He's such an asshole," she purred. "If you'd like, I can claw his eyes out. They'll grow back, but at least something pleasurable can come out of this whole stupid situation."

When Lucifer glared down at her, she turned around, flicked her tail, and sauntered down the hallway.

I sat down on the bed heavily, as if everything started hitting me. My whole world had turned upside down…and I didn't have a chance to tell Parker where I was going! What if he stopped by my apartment? Was this all a dream? A talking cat, the fucking devil…

If that wasn't delusional, I didn't know what was.

Feeling my chest tighten, I leaned forward, placing my elbows on my knees and my head in my hands. I needed to calm down. "None of this is real. None of this is real," I chanted, squeezing my eyes shut.

"Love, this is very much real. The sooner you accept it, the quicker we can solve the problem at hand. Right now, every supernatural being out there is chasing us. I have yet to figure out who put a bounty on my head."

I looked at him and groaned. "Oh god, you're still here."

Lucifer gave me an aggravated frown. "Of course I am! I don't disappear just because you wish it." He held his hands out to his sides. "I'm here to annoy. It's one of my best qualities."

"If you wanted to know who put the bounty out, why didn't you ask one of the demons?" I raised my eyebrows in question. "That would have been the logical choice. Instead, you fried them like bacon."

He clapped his hands, startling me. "Oh! Let's make breakfast for dinner. That sounds splendid." He spun and headed toward the kitchen.

I growled. He only responded to certain things in a conversation, and those were the things that benefited him the most. Shaking my head, I decided to follow him, then stopped, my gaze going to the box sitting on the dresser. Maybe I'd look at the book one more time.

Walking over to the box, I opened it. The book wiggled, bumping around. I lifted the cover. The first page was blank, but writing slowly started to form.

Don't let him take me.

I quickly closed it and stepped back. The box began to bounce up and down on the dresser. When I heard footsteps coming down the hallway, it stopped moving. I turned to see Lucifer standing in the doorway, a questioning look on his face, arm resting against the doorframe. Why did he have to have a sexy five o'clock shadow? It just made me want him even more. My hormones had held off so far because of my annoyance and anger, but right now, I wanted comfort. I wanted the scent of a man. I wanted strong arms around me.

Shaking my head, I walked toward him and bent under his arm. He grabbed my bicep with his other hand.

"Everything all right?" he asked.

Nodding, I forced a smile. "The book is strange. It acts alive."

"It *is* alive. It has many souls in it."

"In it?" I asked, refusing to believe there were actual souls inside of it.

Nodding, Lucifer grabbed my hand, leading me down the hallway. "Oh yes. It's a prison for souls." He pointed to a barstool at the breakfast bar. Reluctantly, I sat. "Aden will be here momentarily. We should have more information then. Hopefully. Depends on his mood. He can be a real dick sometimes."

He went to the fridge and pulled out some eggs and bacon. He examined them, probably for the expiration dates. I wanted to chuckle. Who would have thought the devil would be concerned with the freshness of food?

"I can't tell the date on this one. I'm not a fan of smelling meat to make sure it's fresh. Want to do the honors?" he asked, tossing the package onto the counter in front of me.

"Uh… Sure, I guess." I opened the bacon and examined it. It seemed okay. When I took a sniff, there wasn't a foul odor. "I think we're good."

Satisfied, Lucifer reached into the cabinet, pulling out some pants and holding them up. "Hmm, I've been looking for these." He chuckled, placing them onto the counter.

I furrowed my brows as he started digging for pans. The kitchen was small, so it was almost comical watching him maneuver around with his six-foot-three height. He was almost a giant compared to my short five-foot-three.

As I practically drooled over his well-formed muscles and movement of his tattoos as he walked around the kitchen, I suddenly realized he was still in his damn speedos! Why didn't this concern me more? It wasn't something a man should wear just walking around. They made me slightly uncomfortable and left very little to the imagination. Yet here I was, hanging out with a strange man who strutted around in a pair. And they weren't even a normal pair!

"My ass looks rather fine in these, yes?" he asked, obviously catching me ogling him, then he actually made each butt cheek bounce.

"I'm not sure what to say right now."

"Say you're turned on."

"I am not," I denied.

"If we're going to have a conversation, I hope you plan on putting clothing on, Lucifer."

I gaped as a man in a white suit appeared, his blond hair swept back, similar to Lucifer's. He was especially handsome, but in a pure, angelic way. I was almost afraid to look at him, but something told me to keep eye contact.

Lucifer frowned. "Maye, my brother, Aden. Be sure not to say his name in vain!" He chuckled when Aden shook his finger at him. "What? I only warned her."

"Don't listen to him. He's been out of control for far too long. I had hoped hanging out with you would straighten him out a bit, but he only seems slightly calmer than usual." He eyed me, as if debating whether I was worth his time. I felt like he was a lot stronger than he looked. The fear resonating in me was completely justified.

Lucifer rolled his eyes, then jumped back when grease from the bacon popped at him. "That almost took out a nipple!" He reached for an apron hanging on a nearby wall. "Good thing I've come prepared." He waggled his eyebrows at me. I couldn't help but smirk.

Aden sighed. "Now that Lucifer has put on something, we can finally discuss what has been happening. These details will help you in your mission. I don't want anything to happen to Maye, Lucifer. So stay focused. And don't sleep with her."

"I plan on it—" Lucifer began.

"I *will not* sleep with him."

I stared at both men as if they'd grown horns. Dear gods, one of them was the damn devil, who probably did have horns, and he wanted to sleep with me!

I slid off the barstool. "I'm leaving."

Aden suddenly appeared in front of me, glowing brightly, making me let out a small scream. "Have you ever wondered why you are able to see more about a person when you touch them? Why some people are more evil than others? I bet you have many unanswered questions. For example, you probably want to know who your father is, correct?"

"Ah gods," Lucifer groaned. "There he goes with the glowing again."

Aden shot him a glare before turning back to me. "I have these answers, if you care to know them."

CHAPTER EIGHT
LUCIFER

Waiting for Maye's reply, I watched the two of them, a spatula in my hand. More popping from the bacon had me jerking back. I flipped it, then returned my attention to Aden, who appeared to be getting impatient.

"Well? Do you want to know the answer to these questions or not?" His voice had started to get a god-like quality to it, which meant he was getting angry. That was never a good thing. He treated most people like children. It was never good when he became pissed off.

Maye sighed, running a hand through her hair. "I do..." Then she glared at him, "but not from an asshole like you. You seem to be full of yourself. I mean, Lucifer has an ego the size of Egypt..."

I smiled wide. *I'm glad she notices!*

"But yours is massive," she continued. "Maybe even bigger than the universe. You need to learn how to talk to people. You can't just command them to do something. If you want respect, you have to earn it."

"Oh snap," I whispered.

"Shut up, Lucifer." Aden rubbed his chin with his thumb and forefinger. "That's a little disrespectful on your part, as well, don't you think? I asked a question, yet you think it's acceptable behavior to ignore it? That I am supposed to guess what's in your head? I was trying to be polite and offer you answers to some of your questions."

"Looks like both of us are assholes then." She looked him up and down. "Who are you supposed to be? A god?"

"I thought she almost said—" I began.

"Lucifer!" Aden shouted.

"Said what?" Maye asked, looking between us both.

Aden glared at me, clenching his fists. I could tell he was seconds away from taking me down. He wasn't kind when angry. The pain he inflicted was something you never forgot. It was burned into my mind, yet I challenged him on almost everything.

Aden waved her off. "Never mind. Do you want to know or not?"

"*I* want to know, so do tell, brother." I was impatient. Ten minutes had gone by, but I had yet to learn any information. How much longer did I need to wait to know why I was even here?

Aden walked to the breakfast bar and sat. "Pour me some coffee."

"Please," I said.

Aden raised an eyebrow. I sighed, walking over to the coffee maker to pour him a cup. "So, explain. I can't handle the suspense anymore."

Maye walked to the other side of the kitchen and leaned against on the counter, arms crossed. She wore a pair of dark, ripped, boot-cut jeans. Her tight, black shirt was, unfortunately, too dark for me to see every curve. I would have to suggest some lighter colors to see if she'd wear them. I wanted to see more, but knew she would probably never try on the swimsuit I asked Blake to bring. Of course, my daughter was annoyed at having to purchase it in the first place.

A knock at the front door had us all turning. Other than Blake, no one was supposed to know about the safe house. When I glanced out the front window, I saw Blake standing there, groceries in hand, tapping her foot, looking beyond irritated.

I opened the door and motioned Blake inside. She glanced at my attire as she walked past, rolling her eyes. She was half-demon/half-vampire. Her mood was often grouchy, but she got that from her mother. At least Blake knew when to joke around, though she tended to stay serious around me.

My daughters were the ones who actually took down an organization run by my brother, Nick. He was known for taking innocents and using them for dreadful purposes. Not even I approved of it, but that didn't matter to Nick.

I had three daughters…Jacey, Sin, and Blake…all of whom were similar to me in personality, though Blake usually spent most of her time pissed off.

Jacey commanded the shadows, which were feared by a majority of supernatural beings, and for good reason. Sin led the reapers. She was Death, and very powerful. Then there was Blake, who helped her husband run the vampires in the state of Michigan.

I was proud of them for their accomplishments. The world was better off with them.

"Maye, allow me to introduce you to my daughter, Blake. She's temperamental, so tread lightly," I warned.

Blake shook her head. "Don't even listen to him." When Maye smiled, Blake looked at her more seriously, eyes narrowed. "Not even joking. *Never* listen to him. More often than not, everything out of his mouth is shit."

I gasped and shook my head. "Dear gods, girl. You are giving a bad impression. I happen to like this one, so don't blow it for me. What if I came over to your place during romantic moments with Eli? How about I wake up the baby? Hmm?"

Chuckling, Blake set the groceries onto the counter, then glanced at Aden. "He *does* like this one. He usually jokes around, but he's seriously pissed off right now." She grinned, heading back toward the door. "Peace out! Have fun hiding and shit." She closed the door behind her.

"She's not even concerned for your safety?" Maye asked, flabbergasted. "If I had family involved in what you seem to be, I would definitely be worried."

"Speaking of family, your father would like to meet you."

Aden obviously decided he wouldn't ask if she wanted to. Though it was her fault she took too much time replying. He did give her a chance to say no, but Aden usually did whatever he wanted to, no matter the consequences. If it was in his best interest to have all the dirty details out on the table, that was what would happen.

Maye glanced at me, eyebrows raised. When I shrugged, she returned her gaze to Aden. "My dad is dead. He died when my mother did."

"That was your step-father, which you already knew. Stop fighting me on the information. Whether you want to know or not, I *do* plan on telling you." Aden swept his hand to the side. Gasping, Maye floated over and sat on a barstool next to him at the breakfast bar.

He smiled as Maye's eyes narrowed and darkened to a navy blue, reminding me of the dark storms off the coasts. She was about to lose her temper, and after feeling her strength earlier, I wasn't sure what to expect.

"Your father is Anubis. Have you heard that name before?"

"Finally! I've had to keep my mouth shut this whole time. I'm surprised Lucifer hasn't figured it out yet," Cleo said, jumping onto the counter and snatching a piece of bacon from the plate. When I reached for her, she jumped off, prize in her mouth, and ran to the back of the house, laughing the whole time.

"Cat feet on the counter is disgusting! And you stole my food!" I shouted, bending over to pick up a piece of bacon that fell during Cleo's escape.

"Fucker!" she yelled.

"Oh, my gods, Lucifer. Do *not* bend over in that speedo again. I beg you." Aden squeezed the bridge of his nose as he took a deep breath. "I've never been so disgusted in my life."

"Have you heard of twerking?" I asked.

Aden pointed at me. "Don't you dare."

"As you were saying?" Maye prompted. She gave me a shy smile and looked back at my brother.

"As I was saying, you're the daughter of Anubis."

"And you're also the Keeper of Souls," a voice said from the front of the house.

"Now it's a party! Tell me you brought the liquor, Anubis." I grinned at my old friend as we high-fived.

Maye screamed, leaping off her stool. She ran behind the island, her beautiful eyes wide with fear. When I looked at her, confused, she pointed to Anubis. He started laughing so hard that he bent over, pressing his hands to his knees. Then it dawned on me. He wore the damn jackal head. I had to admit, even I was disturbed when he first started wearing it. These days, he only wore it to scare people.

When he calmed down, he straightened and blew out a breath. "I'm sorry, daughter. I only wanted to show you a bit of myself." Anubis removed the head and set it on the counter. Now she could see he looked more human. His jet-black, spiked hair, the very same blue eyes she had. They looked so alike, it was obvious she was his daughter.

I think Maye realized it, too, because she stood there, staring, not responding to him. After a few minutes, I walked over and touched her arm, earning me a glare.

"I'm fine," she snapped.

Anubis smiled, flashing amazingly white teeth. "Has a temper on her, just like her mother."

"The whore you slept with?" Anput appeared behind Anubis.

I threw up my hands. "Dear gods, is this a family reunion? I was trying to cook a meal for myself and Maye, then you all have to appear and make yourselves at home."

Aden chuckled. "Everyone wants to meet the daughter."

"My mother is not a whore." Maye stepped toward Anput, her fists clenched. "I dare you to say it again."

Anput was every bit a goddess. Her long hair shiny and straight, Egyptian features perfect, dark eyes filled with hatred. "Your mother should have died when she was pregnant with you," she hissed.

Spinning around, Anubis flicked his hand, sending Anput across the room and into the wall of the living room. "You *do not* talk to my daughter that way. Some have died for lesser things."

"You protect the whore's offspring?" she asked, climbing to her feet.

"That's it."

Maye's eyes turned dark black, the white disappearing. I stepped back, a bit surprised. When things in the room began to shake and lift into the air, I reached out, touching her arm.

"Get the fuck away from me, Lucifer." Her voice was low and threatening.

"Sorry. No can do, love. Time to calm down. I know Anput is a bitch, but we can't have you destroying Blake's safe house. She will kill me and not do any more favors for me, which I cannot allow."

It was obvious Maye held power, but we had to figure out the extent of it before something bad happened. I glared at Aden. I could wring his neck. We should have discussed everything before he threw me into the mix.

Maye strode up to Anput and growled, "I should kill you."

"Your mother slept with my husband. I am allowed to be angry!" She shoved Maye back.

"Why did you follow me, Anput? You out to create drama?" Anubis flicked his hand again, throwing Maye onto the couch. Her power broken, things in the room crashed to the floor. She cried out in anger, struggling against his power.

He grinned, raising an eyebrow at me. "Powerful thing, isn't she?"

"I wouldn't laugh at her." My eyes widened when Maye groaned and slowly stood, body shaking against Anubis' power. "Now you've pissed her off more."

"So I did." He sighed. "Look, Anput, this is not your business. I will see you at dinner when our company comes over." He snapped his fingers, and the goddess disappeared.

He turned to Maye. "If you don't learn to control these newfound powers, you will harm somebody, which will not be good for you." He turned to my brother. "Aden is not forgiving."

"No, I'm not." Aden stood. "Enough of this. I've come to let you know that someone is out to get you, Lucifer. You took his soul and he wants it back, doing everything he can to get the book. People will die until he finds it. At the same time, he has somehow convinced demons and other supernatural beings to take you out. I have yet to find out what he has offered, but if they are willing to go against someone as strong as you, it must be good."

"You can take care of this with a snap of your fingers," I said to my brother. "Why not end it now?"

"I don't know who is behind this, but whoever it is, they have substantial power. I know it can't just be the human who wants his soul back. Plus, I allow humans to have free will, which means I don't stop them from making choices. I just guide them the best I can and watch."

"That's fucked up." Maye shook her head in disbelief. She didn't look like she was struggling against Anubis anymore. "You have the power to stop this, but you won't?"

Aden shrugged. "It is a promise I have made mankind. They are allowed the freedom to make their own choices in life."

"You are all messed up in the head. I can't believe you would do this to us! We can't live from day to day wondering what psychopath will take us out."

Again, Aden shrugged. "There is much more for you to know, but I will leave your father to explain it. I have a lunch meeting." Then he was gone.

Even though he didn't show it, my brother cared far too much. He even influenced situations more than he should. He brought me in to help Maye when he could have stood by and done nothing, perhaps watching her die.

Anubis yawned. "I may take a nap before explaining."

"Oh no, you don't! You will stay here and explain everything. If you don't, my life's mission will be to hunt you down," Maye threatened.

He glanced at me. "She reminds me so much of her mother. The first night we met, she threatened to kill me." He sighed happily. "Love at first sight. I was sad when she passed away."

Maye looked away as tears formed in her eyes, her chin trembling. "And you, a god, could have prevented that."

"How do I stop a car accident?"

"What good are you if you can't save a life?"

Anubis gazed at her, Maye glaring back. When he didn't respond, I smirked and nodded.

"One point for Maye. Zero for Anubis."

CHAPTER NINE

MAYE

I glared in Lucifer's direction, then walked toward Anubis. "Why were you not in my life? Why didn't you take care of us?" she demanded, shoving him hard.

Anubis stumbled back a step. "I'm a god. We do not hang around with our lovers. Plus, Anput found out. After that, I was lucky if she let me out of her sight. She was so angry. Still is, as you just saw. If I continue to put you before her, she will cut my throat in my sleep."

"Sounds like a psycho." I shook my head, glancing over at Lucifer, who had started picking things up from the floor. It was scary to know I wielded such power, and the fact I had no idea where it came from, but I didn't want to focus on that. Right now, I was angry at my father for his abandonment. Was he just here to ruin the quiet, private life I had managed to scrape together after my mother's death?

Hearing a noise coming from the back of the house, I recognized my cell phone's ringtone. Since not many people knew my number, it was probably Parker. Ignoring Lucifer and Anubis, I headed in that direction, then heard my father chuckle. The asshat acted as if my feelings didn't matter. Or was that how gods really were? That was how they depicted them in movies. They only cared about themselves, then came around at the most inconvenient moments. I really just wanted to go back to my normal life.

Grabbing my cell from the nightstand, I pressed the answer button. "Hey, Parker."

"Where the *fuck* are you? I came by to pick up your new painting, but you're not home. I must have it today because the show is tomorrow night. My assistant is having a meltdown because the piece isn't already at the gallery." Parker's annoyance was typical. Tantrums were part of his flashy personality.

"I'll drop it off in about an hour. I'm not sure I want you to use this one, though. It's…not the same as the others." I frowned, looking over at the covered canvas. I wanted to keep the painting of Lucifer for myself, but how would I explain that? I wasn't supposed to like him, but an artist should be able to keep some of their art, right?

"Girl, if you want money, you will let me have that piece. If you're reluctant, it has to be a good one. One hour, honey, or I'm going to hunt you down."

He hung up without saying anything else. I set the phone back down, debating on how to explain to Lucifer that I needed to leave, not to mention with a painting that looked exactly like him.

When I turned around, I jumped, Lucifer leaning against the doorframe. At least he had put on jeans and a t-shirt. I examined him silently, wondering if he could tell that I was attracted to him. When he started toward me, I took a step back, holding up a hand.

"What are you doing?" I asked.

Lucifer shrugged. "Just wanted to make sure you were okay. I know it's a lot to take in, even for me. I didn't know this was going to happen. Hell, I thought you were just human."

He ran a frustrated hand through his hair.

"I'm concerned about you, Maye. I remember when Blake learned about me and her powers. She didn't handle it very well. She was in denial and very angry. I can only imagine how you must feel. Tell me what you're thinking."

When I didn't respond, he raised his eyebrows in question. Finally, I mumbled, "You make me uncomfortable."

He cocked his head, smirking. "I do? Why?"

I swallowed. "Isn't Anubis waiting for us in the kitchen?"

Nodding, Lucifer kept walking toward me, forcing me back against the dresser. When I tried to step away, he placed his hands onto the top, boxing me in with his arms, and grinned.

"I know you want me," he purred. "I can smell it."

"Very big ego. Very, very big ego."

I averted my gaze, my body heating. His blue eyes, so hypnotizing, were hard to miss. I didn't know if I could hold out against him. Why did he suddenly try to pursue me? What had changed in the last few hours?

"Oh, my gods. Get a room." Cleo walked in and prowled around the room. "I didn't agree to this assignment so I could watch you two play kissy-face. I might actually barf. Knowing Lucifer as long as I have has made me realize how much of a man-whore he is. If he could catch a sexual disease, this man would have several of them."

"Oh, shut up, Cleo. From what I remember, you had a harem of men. Do not scold me for liking the female form." Lucifer moved away from me, the spell broken.

I cleared my throat. "Anyway… Anubis? You left him alone in the kitchen?" I hurried out of the room, disturbed by what happened. Would he have kissed me? I frowned, confused.

Lucifer followed, chuckling. "This is not over, Maye."

"If you say so." I quickened my pace, finding Anubis sitting in the kitchen, eating.

He raised his fork in greeting. "This is good. Cook some more, Lucifer!" He shoveled another forkful of eggs into his mouth and moaned in appreciation. "I don't get food like this at home. I need a new cook, but everyone is afraid of me." He furrowed his brows, as if confused.

"Could it be because you're a *god*?" I asked, hopping up onto the counter to watch him eat. The man must have been starving because the second Lucifer picked up the plate of bacon, he motioned him closer and grabbed a few pieces.

"No. It's because I am the God of the Dead. People do not want to be around someone responsible for the dead. It doesn't sound too…friendly."

"So, why are you here?" I asked, wanting to get this conversation over with. I felt like we were sidestepping the topic, but avoiding confrontations must have been a god thing.

Anubis sighed and set down his fork, leaning back in the barstool before he realized it didn't have a back to it. "You are the Keeper of Souls. That means the book Lucifer has is now yours. It was decided, since Lucifer is obviously not keeping good track of it…" He glared at him, "that you were to be responsible for it. The souls need protection, need someone who can control them. It would be disastrous if the book fell into the wrong hands. The souls could be released to cause havoc among the humans."

We heard glass shatter at the back of the house. We all raced to the bedroom, seeing the window broken out, glass littering the floor. But what caught my attention was the box tipped over on the bed, the book gone. Fear clenched my heart at the fact the one person charged with protecting it, me, had failed.

Quicker than I'd ever seen somebody move, Lucifer ran and jumped out the window. I bolted to it to look outside. I saw him standing there, looking around, hands clenched.

"There are too many people around. I don't know who it was," he growled. "How did they know we were here? I made sure no one followed us."

Anubis stood behind me. "You're the Keeper of Souls, Maye. It's time to do your job."

"I don't *want* this job."

"There's no way to stop it now. You're the Keeper, so you must find the book. You are running out of time. If they figure out how to release the souls, the world will devolve into chaos. Not even Lucifer or I will be able to stop it from happening."

His jovial mood has disappeared, replaced with an imposing seriousness. I wanted to hide from it all, but he suddenly smiled.

"I think you'll be fine." Then he was gone.

*

Blake watched the camera feeds, then pushed a button to freeze the screen. Lucifer paced the living room. He was angry. There was no joking with him as he impatiently waited for Blake to show him the security tapes.

"I thought your windows were bulletproof." Lucifer shook his head in anger. "I was careful. There is no reason for someone to break into this place."

Ignoring him, Blake pointed to the computer screen. "Does he look familiar?"

He leaned over her shoulder. "Yes. That's Ace Benson. I have his soul because he is due to die soon. Though I find it odd how young he looks."

"How long ago did you take his soul?" Blake asked, tossing her hair over her shoulder. She was eerily like her father. Their mannerisms, their looks… I wondered if they realized it. I thought mentioning it would probably get me punched by one or the other, perhaps both, so I kept my mouth shut.

"Well, it's probably been nearly sixty years ago. He was only twenty at the time. Considering he should be nearly eighty, why does he look to be only thirty in the camera footage?"

Blake nodded. "I would say something supernatural is on his side, someone extremely powerful." Blake frowned, tapping her bottom lip with her finger. "This is bad, Lucifer. You have demons and a human after you, but now someone else is involved? Do you have any clue who?"

He shook his head. We needed more information before the trail went cold. But Lucifer seemed satisfied with the information he had.

"At least I now know where to start." He looked up at me with a feral grin, making me shiver. "Ace has no idea what he just did."

I did not want to know what he planned. Judging by the expression on his face, I knew it would be something destructive. Would Aden approve? Probably not. But did I have a choice in whether I helped him? That would be a no. I was the Keeper of Souls, and despite my reluctance, it sounded like I had no choice. What happened if I ran away? Could they find me? Considering they were all gods, I had to think the chances were exceedingly good.

Sighing, I sat down in the chair across from Blake. She looked at me for a few long seconds, then smiled, which appeared forced. "Look, I know this is a lot to take in, but you're doing just fine. You haven't freaked out and run away yet." When I didn't respond, she grinned wider. "The thought has crossed your mind, though, hasn't it?"

Lucifer wasn't even paying attention, looking to be deep in thought, but I nodded so he didn't hear.

Blake nodded once and closed her laptop. "I understand, believe me. Though I have known about the supernatural world all my life, I just learned about Lucifer not too long ago. It was a shock, that's for sure. Just take a deep breath, think about everything, then let yourself see that you *can* do good for this world. That with your influence and watching over the souls, you can make sure evil stays in Hell, where it belongs."

Hearing her tell me her thoughts kind of opened my mind up to it. Maybe I should look for the positive in it instead of thinking of ways to run away from the situation. But who really wanted this kind of responsibility? Who wanted to deal with someone like Lucifer all the time?

I glanced over at him at the same time he looked at me. He smiled, giving me a wink. I trembled, unable to control how he made me feel. And he wasn't even doing anything! Was it some devilish trick?

"Gross," Blake groaned. "I can see something starting to happen between you two. Listen, Maye. All of us have some kind of influence in the world. I think you would be a good addition. If you decide you want to know more, get my number from Lucifer." Blake stood, slipping her laptop into the bag. "Well, you kids have fun now." She pointed at Lucifer. "I don't want any details. Got it?"

Shrugging, Lucifer leaned a shoulder against the wall. "I can't make any promises."

Blake sighed. "This is going to suck. I need to put those wards back up." She headed toward the door.

"They don't work!" Lucifer called out in a sing-song voice.

"They do for a while!" she responded in kind. "Any amount of time will make me happy right now." The door slammed shut behind her.

I laughed. I couldn't help it. They were hilarious together.

I closed my eyes, exhausted. Remembering Parker's phone call, I debated calling him. Instead, I settled on sending him a text, letting him know I wasn't going to give him the painting. I would have another one, a better one, for him later. Just as I anticipated, my phone blew up, but I ignored it, slipping it into the pocket of my jeans. I did not want to start a texting war with my best friend. He was better and a lot faster at it.

"Your friend giving you a hard time?" Lucifer asked, sitting next to me, albeit a little too close. Didn't he know what personal space was? His closeness made goosebumps erupt all over my skin.

"Uh… Yeah. He's just impatient. He thought that picture of you was going into his gallery, but I decided I want to keep it." Realizing what I had said, I gasped and pressed my lips together.

Lucifer bumped me with his shoulder and smiled. "I knew you liked me."

"I do not! I'm not like every other woman out there. You are not 'man candy' to me." I swallowed hard, realizing that was a giant fucking lie. I refused to let him know how I felt, but I could tell by the satisfied expression on his face that he already knew.

"So, let's put that to a test. I kiss you. If you feel nothing, we move on as if it never happened. I won't hit on you anymore. Promise." He crossed his fingers, then crossed his heart with the other hand.

I laughed, shoving him. "Crossing your fingers does not work in this arrangement, sir."

"Come on, Maye. Test the theory. You say no. I say yes. What's the harm?" He waggled his eyebrows. "Are you worried you'll like it and want me to strip you bare?" He sighed heavily. "I want to see you naked beneath me more than anything."

My eyes widened. "Wow."

"I know."

"Do you say this to all women?"

"Not all of them."

"Ugh." I shoved him so I could get up, but he grabbed my arm.

"I'm serious. I don't say that to just anyone. I mean it with you."

"Fine," I say, rolling my eyes as I sat down again.

He waggled his eyebrows again. "Good."

He leaned toward me and pressed his lips to mine. I sighed softly, allowing him to coax my mouth open so his tongue could slip through. This was better than I thought. Though I was determined to not let him know that. When I put my palms on his chest to push him away, his hand slid up my thigh. That was all it took. My hands went to the sides of his face, sliding up, my fingers weaving into his hair as our kiss deepened. When I moaned, he trailed a hand up my side, his fingers brushing my skin.

Reluctantly, I pulled away. "Lucifer…," I breathed.

His eyes darkened as he looked at me. He leaned in again, kissing me several times. "You taste amazing," he whispered.

I wanted more, but he stood, smiling, holding his hand out to me. "We have work to do, love. To be continued."

CHAPTER TEN
LUCIFER

I wasn't expecting the kiss to be that good. It wasn't supposed to be. It should have been like any other, but something was different. More powerful, supernatural. I didn't know how to explain it, so I didn't even bother. She would have shied away in embarrassment, and I didn't want to ruin our progress so far. But did I want to have these feelings for her?

Pushing the thoughts away, I walked to the bedroom to get my jacket and looked into the mirror. Should I change into a suit? Normally I would, but I thought today called for the relaxed look. Plus, I wanted to match Maye. Odd, because I usually didn't care.

Shaking my head, I quickly changed into a suit, then returned to the living room.

Maye stared at me for a few moments before she blinked. "So, what's the plan? Do we need to go to another safe house?"

Frowning, I thought about it, then mentioned the one place I thought was safest. "Maybe we should go to Hell."

She chuckled, then saw my serious expression. "I… I'm sorry. What?"

"Go to my home in Hell."

She shook her head. "Uh… No. We need to go somewhere else." Maye started toward the door and stopped. "Should I have a gun or something?" Her confusion was adorable. The furrowed brow, hands wringing together, eyes darting around… I knew I'd have to work with her on how to use her powers. I could sense all her untapped potential. She didn't even realize how strong she was.

Smiling, I walked up to her and planted a kiss on her lips, surprising her. "We're going to Ace's place. And nope, we have our powers. I'll work with you on how to use them."

"Use my powers?" she asked, looking down at her hands.

Nodding, I motioned her to follow me to the door. I looked outside first, then opened it, letting her pass me. Locking the door, I started down the steps.

"You didn't notice that you threw a bunch of stuff around in the kitchen? Your eyes turned black, Maye. *Black*. That right there shows me you have so much untapped potential. I'll be happy to show you how to control it." I winked, earning an eye roll in return.

"I-I don't have powers," she replied, walking down the street.

Was she in denial? Did she not remember what happened in the kitchen?

Frowning, I jogged to catch up to her. I didn't know where she was going, because we needed to go in the opposite direction. We probably should grab a taxi since neither one of us had a car.

I glanced over at her. "You don't remember?"

Maye stopped and turned toward me, her hands in her pockets. "Remember what? That I started *flinging* shit around the kitchen? Of course I remember that! Do I want to talk about it? No, I don't! I want to go back to my life. I wish I had never picked up that damn easel and book. I thought my life sucked before, but at least people left me the fuck alone!"

She started walking again, so I jogged to keep up. "We have to go in the opposite direction, Maye."

Growling and throwing up her hands, she turned around and started walking again. "Let's get this over with. The faster I can get back to my life, the better. If that means giving up the book, so be it."

"I doubt the book would like that. It appears to be attached to you." I frowned, not liking how true that was. The book was mine, yet it obviously decided it had enough of me. The feeling was almost depressing.

Shaking her head, Maye continued to walk quickly. I let myself fall behind her, my gaze going to her ass. Dear gods, why hadn't I noticed how round and firm it was?

Blinking a few times, I realized Maye had turned her head to catch me staring! My face heated. Was I blushing?! The devil did not blush.

"You were staring at my ass! I caught you, Lucifer!" she shouted, earning looks from everybody on the street. They stared for a few minutes…until I looked at them, my eyes glowing red. Some screamed, others abruptly turned in the opposite direction. I chuckled, loving how it took very little to scare the humans.

She stomped up to me, waggling her finger in my face. "That was wrong. You shouldn't scare people like that."

I grabbed her finger and kissed the tip of it. "You shouldn't shout my name in a public street. Now, let's get a taxi so I can stop staring at your ass."

*

We arrived in the worst part of Lansing. The area where most of the drug dealers hung out. You never heard about those things on the news, though. It was always about the art district and fun things you could do in the city. I didn't like the idea of bringing Maye down here. She was a demigod, but if she got hurt, did that mean she could heal right away? I was afraid to even find out.

"Maybe you should stay at the diner down the street until I figure out if it's okay for you to come inside," I suggested, thinking I was being a protective warrior.

"Fuck that! I refuse to be the damsel in distress. I know how to protect myself. I did it all through school, and I will do it now." She flipped me off and started walking quickly again. Something she apparently did when pissed off.

Striding after her, I grabbed her arm. "Look, the only reason I suggested such a thing is because I don't know how far your demigod powers go."

She furrowed her brows. "Demigod?"

"Yes. Since you're the daughter of Anubis, that makes you part-god. In other words, a demigod."

She hesitated, then started walking again, albeit a little slower. I caught up with her and pointed to a yellow building.

"That's his apartment. Ace is a very bad man, Maye. He has yet to be punished for all his sins. That's why I went for his soul. He kills women after paying them for…things." She scrunched up her face. "He's a sadist. Someone like him should realize he's going to Hell, but if he figures out how to use that book, he will be able to live as long as he desires. We can't have that."

"Since when does the devil care about someone doing the 'devil's work'?"

"That is *not* my work. I would not convince someone to do what he does."

I sighed, not sure how to explain it. Yes, it was my job to persuade people to do naughty things, but I'd never suggest they do something as sadistic as Ace did. Since these women were prostitutes, their murders weren't given the proper attention they deserved, most thinking they brought it on themselves. It was sad, but it was the way of the world. You had the pure of heart, then you had the evil ones whose souls I kept so they would not be reborn.

I looked up at the decrepit building and sighed. If he was home, things would probably get dicey. No one stole from the devil. I just hoped Maye stayed out of harm's way.

Motioning her to follow, we headed inside and up the creaky stairs. When we made it to the top, Ace's apartment door was cracked open, TV on.

"Hmm, this is strange," I murmured and crept closer to the door. Using my foot, I pushed it open the rest of the way and peered inside, debating if I should be cautious or just walk in. I could handle a few bullets to the chest, but maybe it was a good idea to not startle the man.

Once we crept in, we found the place ransacked. The couch cushions were thrown to the floor, desk drawers emptied, coffee table knocked over, garbage strewn throughout. He must not have returned home after stealing the book. At least he had a few brain cells that still worked. But that presented a whole new problem. I didn't know where else to look for him.

"Wow. This place is completely destroyed." Maye shook her head in disgust as she kicked at a partially eaten apple. "It smells really bad in here. I might actually throw up."

I nodded. "True, but this is mild compared to most of the people in that book."

Looking around, I avoided something sticky on the floor and headed into the bedroom. People always hid stuff in their room. Yet when I saw what waited in there, I immediately turned around, pushing Maye down the hallway.

"You can't go back there."

She looked at me, confused, then shoved her way past. Dear gods, why was she so strong? A demigod should not be able to just push me to the side like that! It pissed me off so much, I wanted to stomp out of the apartment. But I didn't. I walked up behind her just as she gasped and placed a hand over her mouth, seeing another one of Ace's victims lying on the bed. Her hair had been chopped off, the blonde strands, mixed with blood, piled on the floor. She was severely beaten to the point of being unrecognizable. Because of his horrible childhood, he beat them to death, releasing all his pent-up anger. It was a painful way to go. It made me sad. Then again, maybe she was in a better place now.

When I was about to turn around, I noticed something on her hand. Despite the smell, I walked closer, swearing silently when I saw the wedding ring. It seemed he wasn't killing prostitutes anymore. Before he had the book in his hand, he thought removing sinners off the street would give him some leniency, but when he realized the book stopped his trip to Hell, he started killing ones who would make headlines.

Maye let out a sob from the doorway. "This is horrible, Lucifer. I've never seen anything like it before. Not even on the crime shows. This is beyond morbid. How can he do this without any remorse?"

I turned her toward me, wrapping my arms around her. When she buried her face into my chest, I kissed the top of her head.

After several seconds, she took a deep breath and straightened her spine, pulling away. "If this is going to be my life now, I need to get over this. I'm sure I'll see worse."

She turned back toward the room. "We need to search, right?" She entered, careful not to step on any blood.

We looked under the mattress, ignoring the mutilated woman lying on top. Not finding anything, we checked drawers, behind pictures on the walls, even behind the dresser, finding nothing.

We walked out of the room and into the kitchen where there was a small, round table. Small, dark, circular spots, obviously where he put out his cigarettes, covered the surface. There were some papers stained with spilled coffee, as well as a matchbook from a strip club about five miles away. Deciding that would be our next stop, I grabbed it, motioning Maye to follow me out of the apartment.

CHAPTER ELEVEN

MAYE

Lucifer wanted to go to a strip club? I thought he was just being a pervert, until he showed me the matchbook.

"We might be able to find a clue. But I suggest we wait until later in the evening when he's more relaxed. Plus, it appears he's teaming up with other lost souls."

I look at him, frowning, wondering how he could know that.

He smiles and holds up the matchbook. "The owner is another one of my 'clients'."

After I agreed, we started back to the safe house, which I felt was no longer safe. Expressing my concerns, Lucifer snapped his fingers. We suddenly reappeared in the room of a damn nice hotel. An *expensive* hotel. He shook his head when he saw me about to object.

"I like the finer things, so you will have to suck it up. I will not stay in another safe house. Plus, it's harder for somebody to sneak up on us here."

He had a point, but I really missed my apartment. Most of all, I missed Parker. I glanced down at my cell phone, noticing ten missed calls and even more texts. When I looked up, I didn't see Lucifer, but he appeared seconds later, my easel and canvases in his hands.

"I'll go get some paint so you can make another painting for your friend." He disappeared, back within seconds. "He can come pick it up tomorrow," he said, continuing the conversation as if he never left. "Though we may just want to drop it off so we can avoid anyone following him." Lucifer stared at the painting of him. "You are very talented. I'm impressed. I look very dashing."

He winked at me, then entered the kitchen. "Would you like a drink?"

Debating, I finally walked to the breakfast bar and sat on one of the stools. These had backs to them, so I relaxed, relieving some of my tension. What I wanted to do was sleep. It felt like it had been weeks since I'd lain down, but I knew it had only been a little over a day, if that.

Setting a glass containing an amber liquid in front of me, Lucifer started humming as he rummaged through the cabinets to see what food he had. I threw back the liquid, enjoying the hard burn that traveled down my throat, then shivered. Lucifer chuckled at my reaction.

"I'm exhausted, Lucifer. I'm just going to go to bed." I stood, stretching my arms over my head, the hem of my shirt pulling up a bit.

His heated gaze on me, he came around the counter and wrapped his strong arms around me, pressing his lips to mine. I groaned my approval. I wanted to do so much more, but I wasn't sure he did.

His hand traveled beneath my shirt, fingers brushing the edge of my bra, sending a shiver down my spine. I moaned into his mouth, pressing my body against his. Feeling his excitement, my body definitely wanted more. When I deepened the kiss, he responded in kind, his tongue brushing against mine.

I yelped in surprise when he lifted me onto the counter, pushing my legs apart so he could stand between them. He grasped the hem of my shirt and pulled it over my head, then smiled as he gazed at my chest. He kissed each breast, slowly peeling down the fabric of my bra so he could trail his tongue over each nipple. I moaned, feeling my urgency growing. I needed him inside of me.

Grabbing each side of his head, I pressed my lips to his, then pulled back. "I want you to fuck me, Lucifer."

Lifting me, he walked into the bedroom. He gently laid me down on the bed and started to unbutton my jeans, fingers brushing my skin. I squirmed, wanting him so badly it almost hurt. Lucifer's heated gaze trailed down my body as he slowly pulled off my pants and dropped them onto the floor. He groaned, smiling, then touched my left hip.

"I love the dragon tattoo." He bent down to kiss it. "Incredibly sexy."

He started taking his clothes off, deliberately, slowly, periodically touching my legs. When he was just in boxers, he grabbed my panties, sliding them down my legs and depositing them with my pants. Lucifer took a deep breath as he brushed the soft skin between my legs. My eyes rolled into the back of my head at the sensations rushing through my body. I moaned, squirming beneath his touch. When he slipped a finger inside, I gasped, feeling like everything became right in the world.

Way too soon, he withdrew to push down his boxers, then crawled over me, kissing my chest and neck. Positioning himself at my entrance, he looked at me, as if asking permission. I bit my lip and nodded. He slowly entered me. I cried out in ecstasy. As if knowing I wanted so much more, he pulled out and slammed into me, moaning out his own pleasure.

My nails raked down his back and I grabbed his ass as he increased his speed, our bodies slapping together. I bit his bottom lip, causing him to growl, eyes glowing red. He slowed his motion and leaned down, kissing my neck, then nibbling the soft flesh where my shoulder and neck met. It sent a delightful feeling through my entire body just as he slammed into me again.

I cried out as my orgasm hit. It was so strong, I felt like my whole body was on fire. I arched my back as a wonderful, warm feeling seemed to move through my veins. With one final thrust, he groaned as he came. Panting, he collapsed on top of me.

"So the devil *does* get out of breath," I laughed.

He smiled. "Ah yes. You zap my energy. I've never felt anything like it."

His smile faded as he squinted, looking over my body. I furrowed my brow. Had some demigod crap happened to me? Did I grow a third nipple? Maybe I looked like Anubis' jackal head. Fear filled me.

"Does… Does your skin always do that after you have sex?" he asked.

I looked down, my body glowing brightly. I immediately pushed him off and sat up. He grunted in surprise, but I ignored it, rubbing at my skin, gold specks appearing and glowing like rays of sunlight.

"What is happening?" I demanded.

"I don't know, Maye. This is a bit unusual." He frowned. "Something's changed, and not just with you." He didn't seem to be happy at all as he hurriedly climbed out of bed and dressed. "It must be related to your demigod powers. But that doesn't explain why *I* feel different."

"Different how?"

When he didn't respond, I covered myself with the blanket. Everything felt strange. I didn't feel like myself anymore. Did sex open something inside me? I looked down at the skin on my arms. The light had started fading, but the gold flecks remained. I suddenly felt the need to run away.

I stood, grabbing my clothes. I wiggled into my jeans and walked out of the room without saying another word.

"I'm sorry," he said, coming up behind me. "I have to figure this out." Then he was gone.

He left me when I needed comfort the most! If you cared for someone, you stuck around, through good and bad. Which meant he didn't care about me. I wanted to cry, but I had to remain strong. If I were a demigod, I had to build a wall around my heart and not allow anybody else to hurt me.

I needed Anubis to answer some questions, but maybe he wouldn't even know what happened. His skin didn't glow.

Also, what did Lucifer mean when he said he felt different, too? He looked fine. Incredibly sexy and magnificent, though a bit out of breath.

I sat on the couch. Yet again, my life had changed. I didn't know what to do now. Maybe running away was the best solution, but it was also weak. You couldn't just run away from your problems, could you?

*

After thirty minutes, with no sign of Lucifer, I gathered my things. It was probably best if I went out on my own. The book was my responsibility now. How I would remain inconspicuous when I was sparkly would be another matter. Maybe I just didn't care anymore.

I looked at myself in the mirror of the living room. Sure enough, my skin twinkled, even my face. It made my blue eyes pop more than usual. Shaking my head, I pulled my hair up into a ponytail, then slipped on my coat. Glancing back at the mirror, I smiled. A forced smile, but a smile nonetheless.

I debated leaving Lucifer a note, but then again, he didn't tell me where he was going. Grabbing the matchbook, I headed out the door. People in the hall barely glanced in my direction, which was probably a good thing. I pressed the button for the elevator.

As I waited, I looked around the hall. This was a really nice hotel, decorated in cool colors with modern furniture. I wasn't sure which one it was since we didn't enter through the front. Did Lucifer even pay for the room? Maybe he had a permanent reservation, considering his track record with women.

I couldn't believe I slept with him. What did that say about me? I liked him. More than I should. We just met, but it seemed like I'd known him forever. I felt like a teenager, dreaming about a future with somebody who obviously didn't care enough to stick around. He ran off like a frightened little bitch once he got what he wanted.

I took a deep breath, willing back tears that wanted to come. When the elevator dinged and the doors opened, I stepped into it and leaned against the back wall.

I was disgusted with myself. I should have been stronger and held out, but my hormones seemed to rage whenever he was in close proximity. I wasn't the type of girl to demand somebody take me to bed, yet here I was.

"How pathetic."

I shook my head just as the elevator stopped and someone stepped on. He gave me a questioning look, but I just smiled in response, hoping he wouldn't try to talk to me.

"Going out to the club?" the stranger asked.

I groaned silently. Of course he'd talk to me. Nodding, I stared straight ahead, hoping that would keep him from speaking.

"You look good. They'll be all over you tonight," he said, smiling.

Turning to look at him, I took in his appearance. About twenty-five, he wore a pair of swimming shorts and a white tank top. Nothing unusual. His slightly messy, dark hair was swept to the side, and judging by his bloodshot eyes and whiff of alcohol I got, he'd been drinking. Had I not been on a mission, maybe I would have made conversation.

Smiling as the elevator stopped on the first floor, I nodded at him as I stepped off. I hurried across the lobby, hoping the guy wouldn't try to stop me. When I made it to the front doors, I glanced behind me, but he seemed to have disappeared, leaving me slightly confused. I didn't know if I should be worried or happy. Shrugging, I walked out of the building, looking around to try and determine which direction I needed to go.

The sun had already started to set, casting an orange glow over the city. People turned to stare at me as I started walking down the sidewalk. I guessed it wasn't every day you saw someone's damn skin sparkle. It wouldn't rub off, so I imagined it was permanent.

"Gorgeous!" a woman a few feet away shouted. "I love what you did to your skin. It's beautiful."

I smiled and thanked her, walking away as quickly as I could before she could ask any questions. How did I explain my skin became this way after I slept with the devil? I didn't need people labeling me as crazy. I'd probably be on the news and social media in no time.

Needing a ride, I pulled out my phone to find the nearest taxi service. I was about to dial when someone cleared their throat behind me. Turning, I jumped, coming face to face with a seriously pissed-off Lucifer.

"Where do you think you're going?" he demanded, crossing his arms.

"If I'm going to find the book, I need a ride." I pressed the phone number for the taxi service.

Lucifer snatched the phone from my hands, hanging up.

"Hey!" I reached for it, but he slipped it into his back pocket and grinned.

"I'll be your ride." He waggled his brows.

I raised an eyebrow. "Oh, we're back to the perverted talk, I see."

"What does that mean?" he asked, confused.

"You ran off after we did the deed, Lucifer. Are you afraid of me latching on and demanding we get married or something?"

He gasped in mock horror, placing a hand against his chest. "Afraid of commitment? I can tell you're the forever type." He winked, then started walking before I could respond. I expected more of a snarky comeback. He seemed a little…off, like he was trying too hard. Whatever happened between us shook him to the core, and now things seemed awkward. How could we work together with this hanging over us? I didn't even know what to say to him now. Instead, I silently followed him as we headed through the crowds on the sidewalk.

"You shouldn't go by yourself. This club isn't a good one. You're a beautiful woman, so who knows what would have happened," he said, motioning for me to hurry up.

Rolling my eyes, I quickened my pace, my heels clicking harder against the pavement.

He glanced down, raising an eyebrow. "Especially wearing *those*. Dear gods, you're going to kill me."

"What does that even mean?" I asked, exasperated.

"Everything about you makes me want to find a quiet corner and have my way with you," he growled. "But we can't do that again. It can't happen."

And there it was. The truth.

I nodded, pressing my lips together. "You might as well tell me it was a mistake. That what we did wasn't supposed to happen."

He spun to me. "It *shouldn't* have! We crossed a line, and now I have to live with the consequences. Your father will wring my neck. I can only imagine how that conversation will go." He sighed heavily and started to walk again. "We are only supposed to work together. Even Aden told me to keep it in my pants."

"Ah, so I am just another one of your conquests? Another notch on your damn belt, right?" I shook my head in disbelief. "I should have listened to my brain when it said you were a fucking jackass, just another man-whore."

Quicker than I thought possible, he grabbed my arms and pressed me against the wall of a building, a squeak escaping my lips. People stared, but Lucifer didn't seem to care. His eyes turned red. "You are *not* another notch on my belt. I don't even wear them." He released me and started walking again.

I blew out a breath and followed. "Don't people usually wear them with suits? I thought it was the suit law or something. 'Thou shalt not wear suits without belts.'"

He snorted. "Aden did not made such a law." He shook his head. "Why are we even talking about this?"

"You don't seem so cheery now. That's okay. I didn't like what we did anyway." I shrugged. "Wasn't that good."

Lucifer spun around to stare at me. "You're telling me that what we did wasn't good for you?" He laughed. "That's not what your mind-blowing orgasm conveyed."

"Eh. It was more like a baby one. I could do better if I did it myself."

I could tell that pissed him off. His shoulders tensed, hands clenched, ears reddened. He was getting angrier by the second.

Just as those thoughts passed through my mind, he grabbed my arm and dragged me into an alley, then pressed me against a wall. I could feel his hardness.

"This doesn't turn you on?" he whispered.

"Does *what* not turn me on?" I breathed, unable to stop myself from rubbing up against him.

He feathered his lips along my jawline and neck, then nibbled softly, sending shivers through my body. I moaned, letting my head fall back to expose more of my throat to him. "When I kiss you here, does it make you wet? Does it make you desire me?"

"No. It does nothing to me, Lucifer."

He chuckled, brushing his fingers along the waistband of my pants. "I don't believe you." Then he kissed me hard, nipping my bottom lip. He soothed it with his tongue, urging me to open up to him.

"Get a room!"

I jumped in surprise and looked down the alley in the direction the voice came from. Lucifer pulled back, straightening his suit.

"Let's go."

We were back to square one. "I guess we're pretending nothing happened again?"

Lucifer scowled, then turned to walk back down the alley. I took a deep breath, knowing I had to focus on our mission. The book was important. If the souls got out, chaos would ensue. I knew that much, even though I wasn't exactly sure how disastrous it would be.

CHAPTER TWELVE
LUCIFER

Maye had no idea what was going on. I left because I needed to think, and when I returned to the hotel to find her gone, I had become even angrier, which quickly turned to worry. What if someone had taken her? I was confused over the panic that consumed me. I didn't even worry this much about my girls. Then again, I didn't know much about Maye's powers just yet. Things were unknown with her. I was concerned like a lover would be, and I didn't like it one bit.

What happened between us in the bedroom was unusual. Were those... Were those feelings? The overwhelming desire to make her happy and show how much she meant to me? The need to be close to her and never let her go? I didn't even want to think about that. The only feeling I'd ever experienced before was anger, and it was far from that. I didn't know how to love, not after what happened with my first. I had learned to keep a wall up for so long, I felt that it wasn't worth getting close to anyone. Just thinking about it was enough to have me getting angry all over again. It was why Aden and I disagreed more often than not. He could prevent certain things, yet didn't.

Frowning, I hurried on, wondering why in the hell we were walking, especially since she wore those heels. They completely turned me on. I would usually be okay with it, drag her into an alley and do what I wanted, but after I felt the walls around my heart start to crumble, I knew I was in trouble. I had to stay away, but dammit! She wouldn't stop pushing my buttons!

Pulling out my phone, I started to dial a taxi. I'd normally just use my powers, but I didn't want to zap her around the city. Every time I did, she seemed disoriented for a minute, and I needed her head clear.

Dialing Blake's number instead, I explained that we needed a way to get around the city. She grunted in understanding, then told me Eli would deliver a car.

We stood there silently, watching people Maye yawned several times, rolling her eyes as I played on my phone. After hearing her sigh for the tenth time, I reached into my pocket and handed her the phone I took from her, watching as she read the news and texted somebody, probably Parker. I seriously hoped she did not inform him of her whereabouts, but I had a feeling she was smarter than that.

When Eli pulled up twenty minutes later, he climbed out of the car, a knowing smile on his face. Blake and her big mouth.

I narrowed my eyes at him. "Tell Blake gossiping is bad for her health. You both need to be a better example to that baby."

Laughing, Eli shook his head. "She just wants to give you a taste of your own medicine." He winked at Maye, whose brow was furrowed, confused over the whole exchange. I would not be giving her details. The less she knew, the better.

He smiled and walked over to the taxi that had followed him to our location. We didn't usually talk much. He normally went into another room when Blake and I started going back and forth…until she got pissed off enough to jump at me, her hands reaching for my neck. The girl had violent tendencies, especially once she became pregnant.

Admiring the car he had brought, I ran my hand over the hood of the red Hennessey Venom F5. Blake and Eli usually desired vehicles that were less…noticeable. I'd have to ask questions about this later. Flashy was a bit much, considering we needed to stay under the radar.

Hell, who was I kidding? I wanted people to see me coming. If the enemy did, as well, all the better. I would take them all down.

I glanced over at Maye, who shook her head as she slipped into the passenger seat. At least less people would see her glittering. It only made her more beautiful.

Shaking the feelings off, I waited for her to close the door before I climbed in and took off into traffic. Heads turned as we passed. I smiled to myself. I liked to be noticed. However, bringing too much attention to us right now could possibly backfire.

Pulling up in front of the strip club, we looked around. She had started to settle into her role as Keeper and became more aware of her surroundings. Whenever we got time, I would have her go through proper training with Blake or even Jacey, though Jacey's shadows may initially scare her. It wasn't every day someone could disappear into total darkness or manipulate the shadows.

When we stepped inside the club, the scent of cigarettes and cheap perfume immediately assaulted us. The music was loud, the lights dim…except for the stage. An overly thin woman with long, blonde hair danced around, but she didn't seem happy about it. No one seemed to notice or care. Her feelings meant shit to them. I appreciated a dancing woman as much as the next man, but not like this. I guessed they always had a choice.

Wrapping Maye's arm around mine, I smiled at the bouncer, who nodded once as we passed. Some couples liked to share a good time in a strip club.

Dear gods, I can't be thinking about relationships. There never will be any.

Needing to get out of my foul mood, I ran my finger down a waitress' arm and smiled. "Hello, love. Can you be a doll and get us something to drink? I would like a B&B…" I nodded to Maye, "and she'll have something fruity."

"No, I won't. I'll take an old fashioned," Maye said. I raised a surprised eyebrow at her, then nodded at the waitress.

Just as we sat, a girl walked up, offering to give us both a lap dance. We shook our heads, but that didn't stop me from watching her walk away. When I turned back to Maye, I saw her scowl in disapproval. Smiling, I leaned forward, squeezing her hand on top of the table.

"We have to play the part, love. You can't look like a jealous wife." I winked at her before looking around the club.

After several minutes, the waitress returned with our drinks. I sipped mine, but Maye slammed hers back. Again, I raised my eyebrows, wondering what was going on in that head of hers. She acted a little strange, but then again, considering what had happened since we met, it was expected.

When the music changed, one girl walked off the stage as another walked on. She was good, moving perfectly with the beat. I was lost in watching her when Maye nudged me with her elbow. I looked in her direction. Striding down the back hall were two men. Normally, I wouldn't have cared, but one of them happened to be another soul of mine, which meant Ace was probably in the vicinity.

She leaned close so she could lower her voice. "Do you know them? They look like the type you would approach."

Smiling, I nodded. "One of them is in my book. His name is Carl." I watched as he took a seat near the stage, motioning for the waitress. When he ordered his drink and she started to walk away, he slapped her ass, laughing when she called him an asshole.

"What did he trade for his soul?" Maye asked, watching him, suddenly sounding very curious.

"He wanted a bigger penis."

When her head snapped around, I couldn't help but laugh. She stared at me, waiting for confirmation. I nodded. "It's true. The man has the ego the size of his new penis."

She rolled her eyes, then finally joined in with my laughter. We couldn't seem to stop. When Carl turned and spotted me in the corner, his smile slid away faster than wax melting under a flame. He knew why I was there, and I knew he would soon be on his feet.

Just as I stood, he had already started back down the hallway. I ran after him, Maye following close behind. I had to give him credit. Carl was pretty fast for a human. But we were faster. It only took me a couple seconds before I grasped the collar of his shirt. He yelped when I yanked him back and shoved him into one of the walls.

"Where do you think you're going, Carl?" I asked, flashing him my best smile.

He swallowed hard, looking away from my glowing, red gaze. I always showed the evil ones my true eyes, but held back on presenting my true self. Most of them died when they saw it, and I didn't want him dead yet. I barely ever showed it because I always took a while to turn back. I enjoyed being free in my devil form.

Carl squirmed, his large, round body trying to move away from me, but I held firm. I motioned Maye to come close. "Maye, if you are the Keeper of Souls, you should be able to see all his sins through his eyes."

She looked into Carl's eyes. After a few minutes, she shook her head and grasped his arm. Immediately, her eyes got this faraway look in them, like she was transported to somewhere else. I became concerned as the minutes ticked by and her face paled further. Whatever she saw was obviously more than I ever allowed myself to see. When I looked into their eyes, I only checked the first layer of their soul. That was usually enough for me to take it.

When she blinked, a tear fell down her cheek. I touched her arm. She flinched, then shook her head and swallowed. "It's okay. I need to see these things. It's part of the job, right?"

Glancing at Carl, I found him smiling, which infuriated me. I punched him in the face repeatedly, bones crunching. Then I let him go, watching as he slumped to the floor. I had never lost my temper so easily. What the hell was happening to me? My anger just boiled over, and I didn't know how to contain it. Nothing gets to me. *Ever.*

"He's evil, Lucifer. Why even bother with a deal?"

"To ensure he ends up in Hell. There is no asking for forgiveness because his soul is already mine." I turned to Carl. "Tell me where Ace is."

Carl just shook his head, hands to his face, blood dripping down his chin.

I held out my hand, a pitchfork forming in it. Carl's eyes opened wide with fear.

"No! It's not my time yet!" he wailed.

I smiled. "You remember what this is used for, right?" Chuckling, I brought it closer to his face. "Remember what it felt like to have your soul ripped from your body?"

Carl nodded, eyes welling with tears. "I don't want to feel that kind of pain again."

"Well, I could give your soul back, but then I'd just have to take it again. It would be your punishment. There is no other kind of pain like it, Carl. So, are you going to tell me where Ace is?"

Again, Carl nodded. "Yes. Yes. He's in a church a mile from here."

I frowned. "A church? Why?"

"He says the devil isn't allowed in there."

I laughed. That was the most hilarious thing I had ever heard. "You have to be joking." When Carl shook his head, I leaned toward him and lowered my voice. "I can go anywhere I please, Carl. Even church." I stepped over him and started toward the back exit.

"You're just going to leave him here?" Maye asked as she rushed after me, glancing behind her to see Carl climbing to his feet.

"He has more time left before he is supposed to die," I replied, not even glancing at her.

"Do you know what he has done? All those poor people he has affected?" She stopped and pressed her lips together to get hold of herself.

I turned around, my expression set. "This only gets worse, Maye. Spare yourself. Tell your father this is not the job for you. It will only bring you pain and unhappiness. Believe me, I have seen far worse than what Carl showed you." I bent closer, my lips barely grazing hers. "I've *done* worse."

"I don't know if I can be with someone like that," she said softly, gaze turned away from me.

I nodded. "I know."

CHAPTER THIRTEEN

MAYE

Ace was smart in thinking a church would stop Lucifer. I would have assumed the same thing, but I guessed there was more to him than we all knew. Lucifer wasn't the way he was depicted in the Bible. I just wished I knew the whole story of how he and Aden were brothers.

As we climbed into the car, I looked at him, swallowing. "Lucifer, you and Aden…"

It was almost as if he could read my mind. "Yes, Aden and I are brothers, but no one really knows how we came to be." He shrugged. "Hell, *we* don't even know. Aden created the world. He created you. I have input here and there, but everything you see around you is his. If you hate something, take it up with him." He flashed me a smile, trying to be funny. I wasn't in the mood.

"Are we having storytime?"

We both spun, seeing Cleo sitting in the back seat, a feline smile on her face.

"Holy shit! What are you doing in my car? No animals allowed!" Lucifer shouted and narrowed his eyes. "You don't have opposable thumbs, so please explain how you opened the door to get in."

Cleo laughed, her fangs showing. "You are as dumb as they come, Lucifer. I *asked* someone to open it. They were scared at first, talking cat and all, but then I meowed and placed a paw on the door. You didn't lock the car, so they let me in." She stretched her paws out in front of her, making me laugh. Yes, she was a bitch, but freaking hilarious. It was exactly what I needed.

"Get out. Go back to the hotel so we can ride in peace. Plus, don't you need to relieve yourself?" Lucifer raised his eyebrows.

"Problem solved. I found a pile of clothes back here. Nice and comfy."

Lucifer groaned, resting his head back on the headrest. "They're not even mine!"

"I'm only doing what cats are supposed to do. If you have a problem with it, take it up with Anubis and Aden. They're the ones who decided I would be helpful." If a cat could shrug, she probably would have.

She was so carefree. I wished I could be like that.

I glanced over at Lucifer. Anger covered his handsome face, eyes flashing. They weren't red, but I could see a storm brewing in his gaze. If he could snap her neck without getting in trouble, he probably would.

Sighing, I turned to look out the windshield. The street was packed, kids running around, wearing costumes. I glanced at my phone to check the date, shaking my head. Halloween. How could I have missed that? Here I was, sitting with the devil. How much more Halloween-esque could you get?

Lucifer blew out a breath and looked out the windshield. He frowned. "What the hell is going on?"

"Halloween," I replied.

"Dear gods, we picked the wrong night to be out."

Cleo stared at all the children crossing the street. "Seriously dangerous. One of these kids could be a victim of that guy you're chasing."

Lucifer looked over his shoulder at her. "I don't see how having you around is beneficial."

"I think I'm supposed to be a cock blocker, but I suck at that. Pun not intended." She licked a paw. "Can we get going now? I have stuff to do. Couple of cats and I are going to patrol town tonight. I don't want to be late."

"You hang out with strays?"

Cleo turned to me, her green cat eyes oddly human. "Not all of them are actually cats. Do you think I'm the first to be put in this damn form?" She hissed. "Apparently, it's a common punishment."

Starting the car, Lucifer drove down the road. We looked around for a church, spotting a large, stone one with a few cars in the parking lot. A giant cross sat on the roof, glowing brightly. It was actually pretty nice, but ever since I discovered my ability to see the souls of people, I didn't really believe what they taught in church. My mother told me there was a lot more out there than the church wanted you to believe. She said it had nothing to do with who they believed in but how it was explained. That they interpreted everything wrong. I didn't understand her at the time, but it all made sense now.

Lucifer parked, looking around. Seemingly satisfied there was no danger lurking, he opened the door, placing one foot on the ground. The cool air swept into the car, sending chills down my back. It made me wish I had a heavier jacket, but then again, I didn't plan on chasing someone around the street. I had hoped Ace would be at the strip club.

I scrambled out of the car. Cleo jumped out after me, as if she would be effective in a fight. I honestly did wonder why she was here. Maybe stopping Lucifer and me from sleeping together really was the reason.

The lights inside were all on, a glow pouring out the windows and onto the pavement. Lucifer took a deep breath and opened the front door. A strange feeling came over me and I looked at Lucifer, who nodded, confirming it.

Something was not right. I wasn't sure what, but goosebumps formed all over my arms, causing the hairs to stand on end.

When we walked in, we found someone sitting on the very front pew, unmoving. We weren't quiet, which meant whoever it was either knew we were coming and didn't care…or was dead. I wasn't really sure what to expect.

Apart from our footsteps, the building was quiet. A piano, as well as some microphones, sat to the side of the sanctuary in front of us. Lucifer walked around front, staring at the person sitting there.

"Shouldn't you be running?" he asked.

He shrugged. "What's the point? They said you killing me was part of the plan, which I didn't know from the beginning. I thought I could free my soul and ask for forgiveness, but I can't read what the book says!" He threw it onto the floor, the sound echoing.

I bent to grab the book, but Lucifer grasped my arm, stopping me, eyeing it carefully. Then Ace scrambled off the pew and snatched up the book again. He headed toward the front door. When Cleo tried to trip him up, he kicked her out of the way. She tumbled away, hissing.

"Fucking cat!" he shouted angrily as he shoved through the doors.

I bolted after Ace, yelling for him to stop. When I shoved through the front door, the brisk air immediately assaulted me, momentarily stealing my breath after the warmth of the church. He was nowhere in sight. Then I saw something white flash around the corner. When I finally made it there, I saw his car already headed down the street.

Swearing, I jumped into Lucifer's car, Cleo scrambling through the window before I took off. Relieved Lucifer left the keys, I hit the gas, yelping at how much it jumped forward. Cleo started yowling, digging her claws into the seat in order to not fly around the car. I tried not to laugh at the whole situation, but my adrenaline was pumping so much that I couldn't stop myself.

"Watch how you're driving!" Cleo screamed.

I hit the gas to merge into traffic. I could barely see Ace's white Escort down the road. When I saw him screech around a turn, I took the same one without slowing, earning some honks from cars around us.

"What do you think you're doing?"

I yelped, jerking the wheel in surprise, and looked into the rearview mirror, seeing Lucifer sitting in the back seat, anger written on his face.

"Stop appearing like that! My gods, I can't handle it."

Looking around for the Escort, I finally spotted it turning a corner just as a cop pulled out down the street. Swearing, I slowed down, knowing this car would immediately attract the attention of the police, especially if they saw it traveling at sixty miles an hour. As they passed, I turned down the street the Escort did, toward the factory district that was full of abandoned buildings.

Not seeing the Escort, I drove down the first street. There were only two buildings, each with empty parking lots. I sighed, annoyed that I lost him.

"We should just head back to the hotel. I don't like this area. Who knows what we will find." Lucifer peered out the side window and shook his head. "You're just as stubborn as Anubis. Never listening, always doing what you want, even if the consequences stare you right in the face."

"Kind of sounds like someone else I know," Cleo snickered, earning a dark look from Lucifer.

"I don't always jump into risky behavior," he said, obviously in denial.

"I remember a time you were nude at a damn baseball game." Cleo chuckled.

"Wait. That was *you*, Lucifer? And you're giving me shit over this?"

Before I could say anything else, I spotted the Escort parked behind a building, almost hidden from view. The white color kind of helped with finding it.

After we parked, I climbed out, then started to move the seat for Lucifer, but he already stood next to me. "I have a bad feeling about this, Maye."

"Me, too, but we have to do it. We need to find Ace before he gets what he wants from the book. We also need to find out who placed the bounty on your head. Ace has support from someone who is making promises to your demons. Are you that eager to lose your throne?"

He growled, standing tall. "I will *never* lose my spot as the King of Hell."

"You don't know that, Lucifer. It could be many gods behind this." When he didn't answer, I knew he was starting to get edgy. He started toward the factory without me. Cleo poked her head out of the car and meowed.

"I'll wait in here. I think you guys can handle this part without me."

I closed the door and jogged to catch up to Lucifer. The second we stepped inside, we were attacked. Lucifer was fast, blocking each hit directed at him. I was not as good, my responses slower. I only took enough self-defense classes to protect myself from the increasing amount of kidnappings in the city. Where the hell were my powers when I needed them?

A kick to the face had me falling onto my ass, the woman laughing. "You're an easy one. I don't know what he sees in you." She bounced from foot to foot, waiting for me to get up.

Annoyed, I stood, anticipating her punch and ducking under it. Then I swung, catching her in the gut. Surprise flickered across her face.

"Stronger than you look. Not human?" When I didn't respond, she struck out again, hitting me in the face. "Neither am I."

I stumbled back and glanced over at Lucifer, who held his own against three people. I didn't know what kind of supernatural beings they were, but I suspected demons because their eyes occasionally flashed another color. Sometimes red, sometimes black.

"He's a bad ass, huh?" the woman asked. "A real good lay, too."

Feeling the fire light up in me, I swung, punching her in the face. Her head snapped back, blood forming on her lip. Then I felt it. The power filled me so quickly it nearly knocked the wind out of me. My skin began to glow brightly. I gasped just as the woman burst into flames, screaming. When I looked over at Lucifer, everyone having stopped to watch, the three demons burst into flames, as well, disappearing.

"Well, that's a neat trick. Couldn't you have pulled that out sooner?" Lucifer asked, panting. "I bet you're fun at parties." He motioned me to follow.

"I would have if I knew I could do something like that. It would have saved me several hits to the face." I shrugged as we rounded a corner.

Ace stood at a table, different candles and bowls containing what looked like herbs surrounding the book on the wooden surface. Beads of sweat formed on his pudgy face.

"Why isn't this working?" he cried, slamming his fist onto the book. It jumped, falling to the floor.

I ran over and picked it up. It whimpered and snuggled into my chest, like a baby. Gasping, I set it back down onto the table and stepped away.

Ace frowned, confused. "Is it alive?"

Lucifer walked around the front of the table, looking composed, as if he didn't just fight a bunch of demons. His hair was perfect, and even his suit was free of wrinkles. I scowled in annoyance, my face still sore from the punches. I wanted to hit him to see if he actually felt any pain, but there would be time for that later.

"So, still trying to get your soul back?" Lucifer asked, using a finger to pull the book over to him. Two seconds later, it slid back over to me. He huffed out in annoyance, but kept his gaze on Ace, who seemed unsure about what was going on.

"I want to ask for forgiveness. I want to go to Heaven," he replied, pushing his hand through his sweaty hair.

"Yet you killed someone and left her in your apartment." Lucifer cocked his head. "That doesn't seem like someone who wants forgiveness."

Ace shrugged. "That's not what I was told. They told me that as long as I felt bad for what I did and learned from it, I would be forgiven."

Noticing something out of the corner of my eye, I turned to see a woman hiding in the shadows. At least I thought it was a woman. The light shining behind her gave me a vague idea of her body shape. When Lucifer caught my gaze, he moved quickly in an attempt to grab her, but she was already gone. The scowl on his face told me he might know something, but he wasn't about to share it in front of Ace.

"'They' who?" Lucifer asked, placing his hands on the table and leaning toward Ace. He appeared frustrated, yet stayed calm. Fire blazed in his gaze as he stared down at Ace. I had a feeling patience was not one of Lucifer's virtues.

"I don't know. They show up in different forms. I don't even know if it's a man or a woman." Ace sighed, almost like he was about to give up on being forgiven. The man was obviously a killer, someone who couldn't stop himself from hurting people. He hoped forgiveness would make it end, but I had a feeling he knew that wouldn't be the case. He needed to be put down for what he was capable of. I didn't even know if there was help for people like him. They usually just put them in jail, keeping them there until they either were put to death or died naturally.

Shaking my head, I pushed the images of Carl's soul from my mind. I wondered what Ace's held? Just as I was about to reach out to touch him, Lucifer grasped my wrist.

"Don't."

"Why can't I see *your* soul, Lucifer?" I asked, staring at his hand on me.

Ace chuckled. "Do you honestly believe Lucifer has a soul? With all the shit he does?"

As he stared at me, something dark passed through the man's eyes just as he gave me a feral smile. "You know, you kind of look like my type."

I shuddered, unable to control my response. Staring down at his grubby hands, I got the nastiest sensation of what they would feel like. Just thinking about it was enough to make me want to throw up. His eyes were sunken, his thin, brown hair barely covering his head. It was almost as if he were sick.

"It's time, Ace."

Both Lucifer and I turned around to see Aden standing there, glowing.

"You can't be forgiven for your sins. You enjoyed the way you felt during the murders. That is not someone who feels remorse. Maybe you felt awful afterward, but obviously not enough to make you stop."

"But I *do* want to stop! I need to be forgiven." Ace let out a sob, falling to his knees in front of Aden. "I'll do anything."

"Reveal the one who is helping you."

"What?! You've got to be joking, Aden! Don't make a deal with him." Lucifer strode toward his brother, but Aden held up a hand. A flash of light threw Lucifer into the wall and held him there.

"I make the decisions when it comes to this, brother."

"His soul is mine!" Lucifer struggled against his brother's power, to no avail. My eyes widened in shock at how much stronger Aden was than Lucifer.

Aden flicked his hand. Lucifer suddenly went silent, his head hanging. I gasped, running over to him to make sure he still had a pulse. Did they even have one? When I found it, still beating strong, I breathed a sigh of relief. I turned to glare at Aden.

"This is going to piss him off. It's bad enough he doesn't even want to be around me."

Laughing, Aden turned his gaze to me. "You don't know him very well. Maybe he felt that way at first, but now…" He shrugged. "Things are different. I promise you."

His smile faded as he looked down at Ace, his head still bowed. "Will you tell me who is helping you?"

Ace shook his head. "I don't even know who they are. Sometimes it is a woman, sometimes a man. I think they can change their appearance, but I'm not sure."

"I guess you should have asked more questions then," Aden growled, crouching down so his face was close to Ace's. "You're a monster, and your type has a special place. I'm sure Lucifer will enjoy torturing you in Hell." He stood.

Ace grabbed Aden's pants with both hands, marking them with dirt, his expression desperate. "You're not going to forgive me? I did what I could. I tried to help. I *need* you to forgive me!"

Aden shook his head in disgust. "There is no helping someone like you. You torment the weak. I do not forgive such things." He snapped his fingers. Ace disappeared.

"That easy?" I asked. "You could have taken care of him a while ago."

"Yes, I could have, but we still need to know who is behind this. Someone wants the book. For what reason, I do not know. They also want Lucifer out of the way, which makes no sense. Maybe it is just to get the demons to do what they want. I'm uncertain." He rubbed his chin, glancing over at his brother.

I walked over to the table to grab the book, but it was gone again. "What the fuck?"

"Do watch your mouth." Aden shook his head. "You're just as bad as Lucifer." He pointed to where it sat on the floor a few feet away. "The book is over there. I had to make ensure Ace couldn't grab it at the last possible moment."

Someone appeared out of the darkness next to the book. I ran for it, but she had already grabbed it off the floor.

"Thank you for getting this. Ace made it so difficult for me. I would have eventually killed him myself because the nasty little jerk was delaying my plans."

"Anput?" Aden said in surprise. "*You* are behind this?"

"Yes. My lover's soul is in here, and he awaits its return." She smiled, glancing down at the book, which looked like it began to struggle in her hands. Glaring at it, she held on tighter until her knuckles turned white.

Angry that this bitch was the cause of my problems, I felt my power start to flow through my body like lava. I wanted nothing more than to make her suffer. Just as light poured from my hands, she screamed and looked at her arm, which smoldered.

She took off running. I went after her, hearing Aden yell for me to wait. But I was focused, catching up with little effort, which should have set off my alarm bells.

She laughed. "Just like your damn father. You don't know when to back off." She turned, throwing orbs of blue light in my direction. I leapt to the side in surprise. What did I expect? She was a fucking goddess!

When I started to run after her again, she was gone. "Fuck!" I screamed.

Lucifer appeared next to me, anger marring his handsome face. It seemed to be his permanent expression when it came to me. "Didn't Aden tell you to wait? Anput *will* kill you!"

"I was trying to stop her. I think I wounded her, though."

"You wounded a goddess?" Lucifer asked in disbelief.

Nodding, I walked back over to the spot where it happened. We found shards of burnt material. Lucifer bent down to inspect it.

"Your power is a lot stronger than I thought, Maye. I wonder if you can damage me or Aden," he whispered. When he looked up, I swore I saw fear.

"I wouldn't hurt you, Lucifer," I said softly.

He stood up and smiled. "Of course not. Why would anyone want to damage such a delicious form such as myself?" He winked, earning an eye roll from me, then leaned forward, brushing his lips against mine. I sighed loudly, almost as if I had been waiting forever for that.

"Dear gods, get a room," Aden groaned, appearing next to us. Lucifer stepped away from me.

At that moment, I had the urge to test whether or not I could hurt Aden. I'd never been more confused in my life, and just when it started to become clear, he interrupted.

Lucifer looked around the dim warehouse, only a few lights on and no light coming in through the windows. He started heading back toward the doors, searching the area for anything that might be a threat.

"We need to speak to Anubis, Aden. Have him meet us at the hotel as soon as possible. Maybe he can help us figure out what Anput is up to."

He shrugged. "I doubt he will act against his wife, even if she's cheating on him. Those two have been back and forth for years about who they're sleeping with. I don't even think Anubis knows Anput is Maye's grandmother."

My head snapped around to look at him. "*What*?! Don't you think I should have known that sooner?"

Shrugging, Aden smiled. "It would have come up eventually." He disappeared.

Eyes wide, I turned to Lucifer. "I hate to break it to you, but your brother's a dick."

CHAPTER FOURTEEN
LUCIFER

Walking into the kitchen, I opened cabinets and the fridge to see what I had for dinner. I usually asked the hotel to keep it stocked. Even though I could just pop in and out of Hell whenever I wanted, it was nice to get away for a while. Truth be told, I was almost afraid to go back home, considering my demons were so easily swayed.

Glancing down at my phone, I saw a message from Alexa letting me know that ten more demons had gone missing. As of yet, no one had threatened to take the throne. They just suddenly leave without a trace. Most of the time, she had issues with giving out assignments because they'd rather take their chances with Anput, who obviously did such a great job in convincing them to get rid of me.

I shook my head in disgust. It was so hard to find good help these days. You would think they'd learn to be loyal after showing up in Hell. Then again, they lived their lives as fools who fell for anything that sounded like a great deal. I just thought I was better at picking demons to serve me.

Bending to look into the fridge, I found some freshly butchered steak. I would usually let it marinate overnight, but I had to work within our time frame. Then again, I could always just order room service, which sounded better than working my ass off in the kitchen.

Placing the items back into the fridge, I walked to the phone and ordered two steak dinners. As I did, Maye walked into the room and sat on the couch, pulling her legs up under her. She seemed refreshed after her shower and putting on her pajamas. She looked and smelled beautiful…and I wasn't just thinking that because her gold sparkles shone in the light. She looked especially cute and innocent, her long, wet hair curling at the ends. I wanted to cuddle with her on the couch and watch a movie. That would be strange behavior for me. I was a troublemaker.

Deciding to change out of my suit, I went into the bedroom where I had placed my suitcase. Since I couldn't just go back home, I had Alexa drop some stuff off. She was the best minion. I would have to give her some kind of bonus.

Just as I fastened the last button of my shirt, I heard a throat clearing in the doorway. I glanced over my shoulder to see Maye leaning against the doorframe, watching me. Her eyes dark and seductive, bottom lip between her teeth. When I raised my eyebrows, she pushed off the doorframe and started walking toward me, hips swaying. The lacy, black pajama shorts she wore were skimpy enough to be boy shorts. As she got closer, I realized they were!

I cleared my throat, wondering what she had planned. She was unpredictable, but then again, I supposed I was, too. I didn't do well with feelings, though. In fact, I did my best to avoid them, yet within hours, this vixen had started destroying the walls around my heart.

Her hand slid behind my head, pulling me closer. When her lips barely touched mine, I felt myself relax into her. Her warmth sent a thrill through my body. I pressed my lips to hers and coaxed her mouth open, tongues brushing. She moaned, urging me on. I wanted to do more with her, but we had room service coming up. Plus, was I ready for more? I didn't like how the thought of pursuing this relationship made me feel when I spent so many years protecting myself from falling in love again.

But when she bit my lip, I was done. I deepened the kiss, pressing my body into hers. I pulled away and flung the covers off the bed, laying her down and stripping her clothes off. I covered her body with mine.

"I'm not going to go slow, Maye. I need to be inside you."

She moaned in response, arching her back.

Quickly undoing my pants, I pushed them down with one hand and kicked them off. Her mouth curved into a sexy smile as she reached down and grabbed me, squeezing. I groaned, eyes closing as she guided me to her. I slammed into her heat, enjoying the surprised squeal. She dug her nails into my back, moans urging me on. I wasn't going to last long, and judging from her panting, she wasn't, either. Just as I felt my release coming, she screamed as hers hit, muscles clenching around me, pushing me over the edge.

As we both lay there, panting, trying to come down from our high, she said something I thought I would never hear again.

"Aman..."

Scrambling off the bed, I looked down at Maye, a knowing look in her eyes. When I didn't say anything, she smiled softly. Something about it was familiar to me, but I didn't want to believe it. It couldn't be real.

"I remember...," she whispered.

"Remember what? Did you forget something at home? Maybe we should go get it."

I hurriedly grabbed my pants and shoved my legs into them, trying to not look at her. Something happened each time we were together. I was afraid to try again.

I spun away from her, hands clenched. "*Please* tell me this is not happening. I can't handle it. This has to be a cruel joke."

When she touched my back, I jerked in surprise. I turned, seeing *her*.

"Tell me what you remember," I whispered, almost afraid of the answer. Did I want this to be true? I wasn't sure. Too much had changed the last few days, and I did not deal well with change.

"I've returned. You seemed so familiar to me, but I couldn't figure out why. I just knew there was something…more. Then it happened. We made love and a door opened in my mind, all the memories flooding back. It was locked away during all my past lives. Yet here I am, centuries later. I have found your arms again."

"This is a joke."

"It isn't a damn joke, Lucifer."

I blinked. "You wouldn't have sworn back then."

"It was different back then. I have grown up in another time, so I know what it is to live in today's world. I don't have to follow those asshole ways anymore." She poked me in the chest. "And you would be an asshole to make me."

"Ah… It *is* you, Adriana. Only you would poke me in the chest until it hurt." I rubbed my chest with a grin.

"I go by Maye now. That's my name."

"Whatever you say. Look, I have somewhere to be."

I didn't know if I could go through this again. Adriana was my only love, the one who showed me there was more to life than damning people. Then she died. Cancer. After all, she was only human. I did all I could to save her, but it eventually took her.

For a while, I hated Aden, blaming him. He explained that he didn't control the way life went. Sometimes he could aid the doctors, but he couldn't speed up progress on learning how to heal disease.

Shaking my head when she called my name, I turned once last time to look at her. All I could see was Adriana. I bet Aden knew exactly who she was. How many times had he put her in my path and I didn't realize it? Anger grew, rage consuming me faster than a wildfire.

Smiling, Maye placed a hand on my arm. "You should be happy, Lucifer."

"I'm not sure I am. I've missed you for so long, but just when I started to move on, you're back. What am I supposed to do now?" Shaking my head, I looked away to avoid the hurt I knew was in her eyes. She didn't understand what I went through to get over her in the first place. I had finally started to believe I could love again. What if something happened to her? How would I survive that?

"We're together again, Lucifer. What else could you possibly want?" she demanded, placing her hands on her hips.

I gave her a small smile. "Oh, there's the attitude I've come to know and love. Here I thought I had shy Adriana, not snappy Maye."

She pinched the bridge of her nose, blowing out a breath. "Look, I realize this is hard for you, but let's face facts. I'm not leaving. I'm stronger than before. We can be together without having to worry about disease coming for me again. Or so I hope now that I'm half-god." She frowned, looking away. "But you *have* been around the last few centuries. Have you been checked for crabs?"

I furrowed my brows. "This is a concern *now*?"

She burst out laughing. "You should see your face."

"Dear gods, what has gotten into you?" I grabbed her, pressing my lips to hers. "I'm glad you're here. It will take some getting used to because it's hard to believe you have been here this whole time. I'm afraid, Maye."

"Are you *kidding* me? You get what you want, but I still have to be in this damn cat body?" Cleo asked from the doorway.

"Don't you have a toy to play with? I refilled your cat bowl. What else could you possibly want?" I asked, annoyed. This had to be a bad joke on Aden's part. What has she done to help out so far?

As if reading my mind, Cleo sat and stared at me. "I made sure you both knew who you were to each other. I saw it from the start. When I brought it up to Anubis, he went to Aden. You know those boys. Always planning everyone's life out. Look at me. I'm a fucking cat."

"I knew Aden did this!" I let go of Maye. "I'm sick of that fool meddling in my life!"

I wanted to wring his neck, maybe worse, but if earlier was any indication, he was stronger than I was led to believe. I wasn't sure how he got that way, either. We were supposed to be evenly matched in power, but something must have happened for his to grow. Or maybe mine had started to decrease.

Fear filled me. What if this was a way for my demons to get my power…literally? If they got my position in Hell, would they also get my powers?

Maye and Cleo stared at me as I worked this out in my head. There was more at stake than I realized. The book may hold all the souls I'd ever taken, but it also held the very first clue to obtaining my power. I had literally attached a piece of my heart to it so it would always remain loyal to me. That would explain why it liked Maye. She was part of my heart. If someone figured out how to open that section of the book, I could be in trouble.

*

When we walked into the living room, Anubis sat there, eating the food we had ordered. Sure, we were good friends, but he should know I didn't like rude behavior. In his mind, everything was his. It didn't matter if somebody else owned it. If he wanted it, he took it.

I glared at him as he chewed loudly, pointing at the food with his fork.

"This is really good."

"Can you at least take off the jackal head?" Maye asked, trying not to stare at it. "It seriously creeps me out. I'm surprised no one has set fire to it yet."

He chewed, nodding. "Oh, they know better."

Shaking my head, I walked into the kitchen to uncovered Maye's food. I could just order more for myself. She sat in a chair as far away as possible from Anubis.

"How can you eat with that thing on? It's like it's a part of you," Maye asked, staring, almost as if fascinated.

"It *is* a part of me," Anubis replied before sticking the last bite of steak into his mouth. After swallowing, he turned to Maye and smiled. "No fear, my daughter. It's just me."

"Sure. I'm being asked to trust somebody I don't know. Interesting logic there."

"Says the daughter who slept with Lucifer. He is known to betray people for his own benefit, you know."

"Hey! I would never do that to her." I pointed at him. "Don't let there be a repeat of Hong Kong."

"That was twenty years ago. I think I can take you now." Anubis winked.

For some reason, though, I wondered if it meant something else.

He removed the jackal head. "Don't even begin to think I had something to do with everything going on. I had no idea someone would be foolish enough to steal the book, let alone attempt to take your throne."

"You act as if you don't know who it is!" I glared at him, angry he refused to acknowledge his wife's part in this.

My friend shrugged. "She is no longer my responsibility. Is that what you want to hear?"

"No. What I want to hear is you're going to help me find her. Not sit on your ass eating my dinner."

He looked at his empty plate. "Oh, I thought this was for me. Aren't you supposed to be nice to company?"

"Not the asshole kind. Do you mind not putting your feet on the table? This isn't your home."

"Nor yours."

"You both need to shut up!" Maye stood, pointing at Anubis. "Did you know Anput was my grandmother?"

"No."

She blinked. "That's a straight, short answer. Want to rethink it?"

It was kind of hot that she took charge. I could feel myself getting excited…until Anubis shot me a glare. He hated being questioned. His ego was bigger than mine most times.

"I said no. If I had known, I would have left her a long time ago."

"You both cheat on each other!" Maye threw her hands up into the air.

A knock at the door had us all turning. Had it been a god, they wouldn't have used the door. We were rude like that. Maye started toward the door, but I got there first, sending her a warning glare. When I swung the door open, I found a man standing there, holding a bottle of wine.

"Oh, you must be who she keeps blowing me off for," he said.

"Parker! Why are you here?" I demanded, glancing over at Maye, who tried to appear innocent…failing miserably.

"With a British accent. Even sexier." He walked in and winked at Maye before placing the wine down on the counter. "Maye invited me because I kept blowing up her phone. It seems you are the reason she hasn't given me any art recently. We need to have a talk."

"Ah… No thanks," I replied.

"We need to discuss some future possibilities. I just need a moment."

The whole thing felt off. This didn't seem to be the same person Maye had told me about. Even she tilted her head to the side, questioning his odd behavior. When none of us moved, Parker smiled, his face beginning to melt off his skull, exposing dead, black eyes.

Maye screamed just as I said, "Holy shit!"

I grabbed her, shoving her to Anubis. They instantly disappeared. I turned around to face the demon, seeing Azael, whom I only reserved for the worst of situations. He was a powerful killer. I tried to throw a punch, but I felt sluggish. He easily grabbed my fist. I attempted to gather my power, but nothing came. I didn't even feel strong enough to protect myself.

"Not feeling like yourself, Lucifer?" Azael asked as he applied pressure to my fist, forcing me to bend my knees. "Anput has already figured out how to take your powers. Soon, the seat in Hell will be mine." He laughed, the rest of Parker's face melting off, exposing his skull.

Azael was scary, even to me. His technique was even better than Alexa's. Why didn't she warn me he had gone missing? It almost made me angry enough to overpower him, but with very little effort, he had me kneeling on the floor completely now. Smiling, he released my hand.

"You killed her friend?" I asked, shaking out my hand.

Nodding, Azael walked over to the coffee table to get some of Maye's food. He popped a piece of steak into his mouth and chewed for a few seconds. "I killed him before you even showed up at her home." He shrugged. "Once the book came up missing, it was easy to see where Aden would head with this. The souls have already been released. You will soon be without your powers, and every sadistic fuck you've taken a soul from will have it back. Things will be different." He chuckled. "More fun for me."

"Are you fucking kidding me? You're letting the souls loose?" I stood, stumbling slightly. How was I supposed to stop them without my damn strength? It was like I was…human! How disgusting could I possibly be?

Azael picked up a larger piece of steak and tore off a small chunk, chewing as he thought. "Yes, we are. You probably obtained most of them illegally anyway. They had no idea what kind of trap they were getting into."

"They're monsters!"

"And *you're* not? *I'm* not?" He tossed the food down and walked toward me, the dark holes of his eyes lighting up with Hell's fire. "It's time to accept your fate, Lucifer." He looked at his hand, which lit up with a fireball, then reached toward my face. Suddenly, he started screaming.

I'd already closed my eyes, accepting my fate. When I flung them open, I saw his body crumble to the floor, engulfed in flames. Maye stood there, her skin glittering like the sun. She rushed toward me.

"Are you okay? Don't you *ever* send me away again, Lucifer, or I will kill you myself."

"If that isn't a declaration of love, I don't know what is." I laughed, slightly out of breath.

"You're right, you fool. I *do* love you, yet you tossed me to Anubis without even asking! Don't you think I want to fight by your side? I'm not the same as I was before. I am just as strong as a god. You saw what I can do to demons. I should slap you."

"I might just like it," I said, earning a glare from her in response.

"Can you please take this kind of talk to the bedroom? I do not like hearing it." Anubis yawned. "All that good food has made me tired."

Maye looked at him, eyes narrowed. "You aren't concerned that Anput is sucking him dry of his power? This could be bad for you, too, Anubis."

He shrugged. "She doesn't bother me. She may be angry that I slept with her daughter, albeit unknowingly, but she's more angry at Lucifer for taking her lover's soul."

"Oh? Who is her lover?" I asked.

"Ashton."

It all came flooding back. The rich man who had everything, yet wanted more. He took from others, despite them not having enough to survive. He stole money, then changed his appearance and name. He deserved to be in jail. I attempted to put a stop to it by offering him a good deal of money in exchange for his soul. He accepted, then went back on his word. He didn't care about anyone but himself. Now she wanted his soul back? After all these years? He was nearly eighty. What was I missing?

"After you took his soul, he left her for another woman. A human woman who passed away as of a week ago. Anput heard of this and decided she wanted him back. He said he would only take her back if she returned his soul. I don't understand why she is so desperate for a man."

Anubis took off his jackal head and set it onto the coffee table. He glanced at what was left of the demon and shuddered, looking at Maye. "Your powers frighten me, little one."

"And you are just now telling me this, Anubis? Don't you think you should have warned me earlier?" I demanded.

He shrugged. "I didn't think it was related. I told Aden. He said you would figure out the details soon enough." He held his arms out and looked around. "So, here we are."

Aden was really starting to piss me off. He knew so much more than what he told me. Now I had to deal with starting to lose my power and the possibility of Maye getting herself killed because she was the only one who could actually protect me! The anger I felt was beyond anything I had ever experienced before. He brought my only love back to me, yet I had to hurdle obstacles just to keep her alive?

I took a deep breath, trying to calm myself. As if sensing my anger, Maye ran a hand up and down my back for comfort. I just wanted to take her away from all this. Now that I had her with me again, I wanted to forget about all of our problems.

Maybe I should just let them have my powers. As long as I had Maye, I could live without them.

Just as that thought crossed my mind, Aden appeared in front of me, anger written on his face. "You will *not* give up!" he roared. He grasped my collar and brought our faces close to each other. "You will not give up so easily just because she is back in the picture. Love is not everything. I need you by my side to keep this world under control. Anput is not a good replacement."

"You're the one who left out details." I jerked away from him, stumbling, catching myself on a chair. "There was so much more I needed to know, yet you left me to figure it out on my own. Now look at me! How am I supposed to stop them when I can't even use my powers?"

"I didn't tell you everything because I am not able to. You know that."

"By your own choice. You have always been so mysterious about everything, rather than saying what needs to be said. Now I have to hope Maye knows her own powers well enough to trap Anput *and* her lover. I can't direct her on how to use them. I don't even know how powerful she is!"

"She burned Anput. That should at least give you a sign of how powerful she is. Since when do gods get hurt by a demigod? They don't."

"Why is she that way then? She can hurt *any* of us. Explain that to me."

For once, Aden looked lost. He shook his head. "I do not know."

I gasped in mock shock. "An answer you don't have? It's one of the most important ones, too. But you could be lying, which honestly wouldn't surprise me."

"I never lie, Lucifer," he growled.

"Withholding information is the same as lying. Stop playing games with me, brother."

Feeling week, I slowly walked to the couch and sat down. All I wanted to do was sleep. Normally I went weeks without it, yet I felt like I could sleep for days.

When Aden didn't say anything, I looked at him, eyes narrowed. "What are you not telling me?"

Maye sat next to me, snuggling into my side. It was nice to have her close again, the warmth of her body comforting me. I wished we had seen each other again under happier circumstances.

As Aden stood quietly, seemingly at war with himself, I admired Maye's long fingers with painted black nails resting on my thigh. She was a beautiful woman, very different from the first version of herself. I liked this dark-haired beauty with blue eyes that reminded me of the ocean. She was rare and gorgeous, the attitude completing the package. I wrapped my arm around her shoulders and smiled. It was good to have her home.

"When you took her lover's soul, I knew they were together," Aden said softly.

Anubis' head spun toward him so quickly, I thought it was about to come flying off his shoulders. Eyes narrowed, he stood.

Aden took a step back, holding up his hands. "She asked me to keep it a secret. I agreed, of course, because I like to keep things in confidence. It has always been a rule when people talk or pray to me."

Scowling, Anubis took a seat again. He still looked pissed, but then grabbed a bag of candy off the table and started munching. Where the hell did that come from?

"Lucifer stole his soul, even though he wasn't nearly as bad as some of the others he has taken. For some reason, Anput felt he was targeted because of her and that Lucifer had reasons outside of what I knew. In my investigation, I found nothing odd about the situation, but she made me promise to see if I could get his soul back. Well, I never did. So when the book went missing, I had my suspicions, but then Ace came up with it, confusing me. When I confronted Anput, she denied it, of course. She hardly ever tells the truth, so I don't know why she would this time." He sighed. "Lucifer, she blames you for him leaving her for someone else."

CHAPTER FIFTEEN

MAYE

I did not want to be involved in family drama. In fact, I had the overwhelming desire to leave. The only thing stopping me was Lucifer. I wanted to be here to support him. I remembered every promise he ever made me. Remembered he asked me to marry him, despite Aden saying it wasn't possible. Remembered how he took care of me as I slowly died from cancer.

It was strange how it happened. I came into my powers as we made love the first time. Then we had sex again, a door suddenly opening, all my previous memories bubbling to the surface. I finally had answers as to why I fell for him in the short span of two days.

Thinking back, the feelings were so incredibly strong. All I could think about as I came was how much I loved him and wanted to be with him always. It didn't make sense immediately, then everything changed. Every memory we shared came pouring out. I wanted him, needed him. Everything about him was mine. I just hoped he felt the same way.

When he put his arm around me, I felt the familiar sense of comfort. As I fell into his embrace, I ignored Anubis' raised eyebrow. If he were being fatherly, I guessed the speed of our relationship would concern him, but judging from the nonchalant expression on his face, it didn't appear to be the case.

"Okay, so she's coming after me because I took his soul…erroneously, according to her. She's pissed off because there are worse people out there I could have taken souls from," Lucifer said. When his brother nodded, Lucifer chuckled. "She's a damn goddess! What would she want with an eighty-year-old man? She can have anyone she wants! Hell, she has Anubis, and I think he's a sexy lad."

Anubis held up his beer, saluting him. "Thanks, Lucifer. That's very kind of you." He took a long drink.

"Where is he getting this stuff?" I asked Lucifer.

He gestured to the fridge. When I still seemed confused, he wiggled his fingers. "Powers, love."

I would never really understand that until I understood my own powers. I guessed they could have anything they wanted with just a thought. Would I be able to do the same? I was almost afraid to find out.

*

We lay next to each other, panting. I breathed out, trying to catch my breath. Lucifer laughed, coughing as he tried to catch his own.

"That was great," I said, earning some more laughter from him.

Everything was scheduled to go down tomorrow. I was nervous, afraid something would happen to Lucifer, especially since he was so weak. What if they took his power away completely? He tried to reassure me, saying that would be a long process because they had to figure out how to release all the souls first. They were getting closer, the souls seeping out slowly, but I knew once the book was torn open, so would his heart. It made me want to cry. Was it as painful as it sounded? I was frightened. If something happened to him, I would hunt Anput down and kill her.

I knew swooning over him made me sound pathetic, but no one understood what we had. True love. He would do anything for me, and vice versa.

"You're mine. Always. If you left me again, I wouldn't be able to go on, Maye." He kissed my cheek, trailing his lips down my neck.

Rolling over to face him, I cupped his cheek, rubbing the scruffiness. He smiled warmly at me.

"I love your lips." He kissed them softly. "Soft and pouty. I could kiss them all day."

I laughed. "You're so cheesy."

"Sometimes."

If it weren't so dark, I bet I could see him blush.

"But I'm serious, Maye. I can't live without you anymore. Having you back in my life is fate. We were meant to be. Why else would the door to your memories open up like this? Who knows how many times our paths have crossed over the years, and it never was the right time." He sighed. "I love you."

"I love you."

I kissed him softly, my tongue coaxing his mouth open. He moaned, running his hand down my side and over my ass. When he gripped it hard, I laughed and wiggled.

"I bet this ass would look good in a pair of bikini bottoms."

"Just like yours do in speedos?"

"Exactly. We can match." He chuckled when I raised an eyebrow.

I laid my head on his chest, listening to his heart, which sped up and slowed down repeatedly. He said it was because they kept trying to release more souls. His nonchalant attitude concerned me. Why were we just lying around? I wanted to get up and search for Anput, but he insisted we had to adhere to the plan. If we didn't, she would have the upper hand.

Deciding to watch a movie until we fell asleep, Lucifer turned on the TV. Just as he was about to change the channel, I put a hand on his to stop him and sat up.

"Look!" I cried.

The camera was fixed on the morgue, people shuffling out the door, looking stunned, some of them sporting mortal wounds.

"We don't know what's happening, but it looks like…like the dead have come back to life! It's like a real-life zombie movie, Tara," the male news reporter said, voice shaking.

"Are you telling me that people who have been dead, possibly for days, are coming alive as we speak?" the female behind the desk asked, surprise flickering on her face. *"Is this a prank, Paul?"*

Paul shook his head. *"Zoom in closer, Dave, so she can see some of the wounds on them. Look, Tara. They aren't even wearing proper clothing."*

I turned to Lucifer, whose face had paled. He grabbed my hand, pressing it to his lips. "Whatever happens, know that I love you, Maye." His eyes fluttered closed and muscles relaxed.

"No, don't you leave me. Don't you *dare* fucking leave me, Lucifer!" I screamed, shaking him as the last rays of life faded away. Not knowing what else to do, I shrieked for Aden.

He showed up seconds later, then shielded his eyes because the blanket had fallen from my chest. I hurriedly wrapped it around me and pointed to Lucifer, tears falling down my cheeks. "Make him wake up. Don't let him leave me."

Aden stared down at Lucifer, tears forming in his own eyes. "I had hoped to prevent this, but there was nothing I could do."

"You can do anything you want to! Stop living by these damn rules!" I shook Lucifer again, to no avail.

Scrambling off the bed, I grabbed my clothes and quickly dressed, not caring how much of me Aden saw. My skin started to glow as my anxiety and agony grew.

When I looked up, Aden was gone. He abandoned me just like he abandoned his fucking brother. I couldn't believe this was happening. I needed Parker. I needed my best friend. Yet when I dialed his number, it went straight to voicemail. Why didn't he answer? Lucifer had tried to tell me something about him earlier, but I was too wrapped up in him at that moment.

Deciding I needed Anubis, I covered Lucifer with the comforter, then ran into the living room. "Anubis!" I shouted.

Seconds later, he showed up, holding a sub sandwich. "Yeah?" When he saw the tears on my face, he immediately dropped it. "What is the matter, daughter?"

"Lucifer is gone. They released the souls," I cried. "Please, help me fix it."

He shook his head. "I am a god. I can't interfere."

"Anput is interfering. Why can't you?"

"Believe me when I say she will be punished, but I can't stop her. The only thing I can do is tell you where her lover lives. You'd have to take it from there."

"Why the fuck is everything like a damn puzzle with all of you? I need help, but no one is helping me! Who made up these damn rules?"

I raked my hands through my hair and started to pace the living room, trying to think of my next move. I didn't even know where to begin.

I turned and glared at Anubis. "Tell me where the asshole lives."

*

He just had to live on the top floor. How the hell was I supposed to get inside? I groaned, not sure I could do this alone. I was used to having Lucifer by my side, but now I had Cleo standing behind me, shivering and whining about being cold.

"Shut up, Cleo," I muttered angrily.

"Chill out. Why are you so damn angry at me?"

"Because you're bitching about being cold. Just go back home then."

I headed to the door and pressed the button for every apartment, hoping someone would unlock the door. Thankfully, it buzzed and I walked in, Cleo scampering in behind me. I started toward the elevator, seeing an older lady walking off. She stared at me, eyes wide, looking me up and down, then glancing behind me.

I pointed up. "My sister-in-law lives here."

She nodded and hurried off.

I looked down at Cleo sitting at my feet. "She was probably wondering who the fuck walks around with their cat." I sighed, using my foot to urge her onto the elevator. "This would be so much simpler if you were human."

Cleo sat down and licked her paw. "I have to serve out my sentence."

"Well, they could at least give me some real help."

I tapped my foot impatiently as the elevator slowly traveled up. I wasn't even sure how many apartments there were, but judging by the buzzers outside, there were a lot. Good thing I got the apartment number from Anubis before he left.

"You can be kind of a bitch, you know that?" Cleo asked, blinking up at me with her large, green cat eyes.

"As can you, so I guess that makes us even."

Once we made it to the top floor, I looked for the apartment number on the door. Whispering the one I needed over and over, I finally spotted it at the end of the hall. I started toward it, but Cleo darted in front of me.

"How do you plan on getting inside?" she asked.

I shrugged. "I don't know."

"Don't you think you should have a plan? He could have weapons or, worse, Anput could be in there."

"I hope to find that bitch," I growled.

Sighing, Cleo walked toward the door. "Knock away."

That sounded too easy. Smirking, I gripped the doorknob, thinking about it just melting away. My whole body heated, my hand glowing brighter and brighter. When the knob fell to the floor, I leapt back in surprise, staring at my hand.

"Well, look at all the tricks you know," Cleo said, staring at the glowing doorknob on the floor.

"Impressive, right?"

"Sure. Show me what else you can do. Does that work on ex-lovers who may have already crossed over?"

"Morbid."

"Says the person looking to kill Anput."

Shaking my head, I slowly pushed open the door with my foot, wishing I had a weapon. I guessed I *was* armed, as long as my power cooperated. I tried not to think about the fact I really didn't know how to use it yet.

Looking around the apartment, I frowned. Empty. What did I expect? It wasn't like they would do it right in his home. Sighing, I walked into the living room, scrunching up my face at the mess. There were cigarette butts and empty food containers everywhere. Some of them still contained food, growing moldy. There were even men's and women's clothing on the floor, as if they didn't get dressed after a night of passion.

Sniffing, I detected a faint, grotesque odor of something I couldn't place. The more I walked around, the worse it got. Debating if I wanted to see the kitchen, I decided to check the rooms first, just in case he left evidence. As I headed down the hallway, I spotted a torn piece of paper on the floor, part of an address written on it. I shoved it into my pocket.

Each room was pretty bare. He didn't decorate, obviously didn't care if anything matched. I would assume he was hardly ever home, except for the empty food containers everywhere.

Cleo came into the back bedroom and sat down. "This place is disgusting."

"I know."

"We should get out of here. I didn't see anything that would be helpful. I thought I'd check out that smell…" Her voice trailed off.

"A body?" I asked.

"Yep. Not sure who it is, though."

I pulled my shirt over my nose, hoping to help with the smell, then walked into the kitchen, gagging at the sight. The body was bloated, seeping some kind of fluid out onto the floor. Since it wore a nightgown, I assumed it was a woman. Figuring out how she died would be impossible. I felt bile rising in my throat.

Spinning around, I hurried out of the apartment, hoping the partial address on the piece of paper would be enough help.

As soon as I closed the door of the apartment, making sure Cleo had gotten out first, I took a deep breath, but I could still smell it in my nose. We hurried down the hallway to the elevator, ignoring one of the neighbors who came out to look around the hall.

Shit, now somebody has seen me here.

I groaned, pressing the button over and over, as if it would help it move faster. Cleo stared up at me with a curious expression.

"You handled that better than I thought you would," she chuckled. "I didn't think you would actually go look at the body."

"I had to see who it was."

When the doors swished open, Cleo trotted onto the elevator. "Hard to say…"

"Too bad everyone who could help me disappeared like cowards. I will never forgive them for this." I shook my head, pressing the button for the first floor.

"Gods can't be involved."

"What if one *is* a god? No one can stop her?" I shook my head in disbelief. "Seems this was just a way to avoid being involved. Unless it directly affects them, they make excuses."

"Lucifer is Aden's brother. Don't you think he would have helped if he could?" Cleo asked before yawning widely.

How the hell was she tired? My adrenaline pumped wildly.

"I don't know, but none of this makes any sense to me. Had it been my brother, I would do anything I could, no matter the consequences."

"So, it seems the apartment was a bust."

"Not really." I pulled out the partial address. It contained the last number of the house and the road name. Smiling, I flashed it to Cleo. "We have this."

CHAPTER SIXTEEN

MAYE

I checked on Lucifer, who still lay quietly in bed. I sat down next to him, feeling tears well up in my eyes. I touched his cool hand.

"I miss you, Lucifer. I wish you were here so we could take down Anput together," I whispered. "I don't know what to do."

Part of me wanted to lay down next to him and forget about everything, but I knew I needed to get my ass moving. No matter how it ended, I was determined to get justice for Lucifer. He might be gone, but at least I could make Anput regret taking him from me. I would make sure she couldn't cross over. She needed a punishment similar to Cleo's.

Cleo appeared in the doorway of the room and stared at me silently. When I gave her a questioning look, she started walking toward me. "If you want revenge for Lucifer so badly, sitting here isn't going to get you there. Stop being a baby and shedding tears over that asshole. He really was a prick." I glared at her. "I'm just saying. You have no idea what he was really like." She looked away. "Let's go down to the road listed and see what's there."

*

It was a dirt road I wasn't familiar with, despite living in the area my whole life. I was surprised Lansing even had a dirt road. It was well maintained, too, with only a few houses. Cleo placed her paw on the paper as I drove Lucifer's flashy car down the dirt. I smiled slightly, knowing he would probably flip out if he knew.

"The last number is nine," Cleo said.

"I hope I can read the house numbers. It's so damn dark."

Cleo placed her paws on the dashboard. "What about that farmhouse? It looks condemned."

Not seeing it right away, I was about to yell at her for messing with me, but then, in the distance, I saw a farmhouse, the white paint peeling. There was a faint glow coming from one of the windows.

Parking at the end of a driveway that meandered through a cornfield, I climbed out, my sidekick following behind.

"I'm not a damn sidekick," the cat mumbled. "I have a name."

"Well, I didn't mean to say my thought out loud. But I was just thinking. What can you do? Do you know karate?"

Joking around was my way of coping. If I didn't lighten the mood, my thoughts would turn to Lucifer. The anger simmered just under the surface.

We heard voices in the distance, one male and one female. I looked down at Cleo, who pricked her ears forward to hear what was said. They were too far away for it to be clear, so we snuck up the road, periodically hiding behind the cornstalks.

"You were using me?!" she shrieked, chasing the man through the door and down the porch steps. "I put my life in danger because of you! You ungrateful douchebag!" Watching him trying to run from her would have been comical had I not been determined to get my revenge.

"I didn't ask you to do this for me. I was prepared to die for my sins, but thank you anyway, sweetheart. At least I can cause some more havoc now." The guy, who I assumed was Ashton, laughed. "I feel like me again! I feel human."

We were just a few feet away. Their voices carried, the light on the porch illuminating them.

"Exactly. Which means I can kill you." Anput shoved him so hard, he fell back, hitting his head on the ground.

"You fucking whore," he groaned, holding his head. "This is why I left you in the first place. You're a damn psycho." He slowly climbed to his feet.

They continued to argue, so I crept along the stalks, looking for a way into the house. All I needed was the book. Lucifer would probably not come back, though. I had the feeling they destroyed the part of his heart contained within it.

Sadness filled me…until I felt something bite my leg. "Ow," I hissed quietly.

Cleo glared. "No feeling sorry for yourself. Time to get the damn book."

"You bit me."

"I know."

I rolled my eyes, hurrying down the driveway. The cornstalks were so high, they wouldn't be able to see me unless they really looked. But just as I passed, Anput's head turned, gaze focused on me. She smiled broadly and brought her hands together, a blue orb forming.

"Welcome, Maye. How nice to see my granddaughter. I'm sorry I don't have any cookies!" She threw the ball. I jumped to the side. It barely missed me, the heat leaving a burn on my leg, despite my jeans.

I cried out in pain, hobbling slightly. "I would be afraid to eat your cookies anyway."

Deciding to try what she did, I closed my eyes and held my hands close together, picturing myself conjuring a bright yellow ball of power. When I opened my eyes, I was immediately assaulted by the brightness in my hands, making me squint. Anput's face fell, then she bolted toward the house.

"Stop!" I screamed, throwing the ball at her.

She cried out as it hit her in the back, knocking her to her knees. She stood, forming another blue ball. She smiled, eyes dark, as she threw it. I moved quickly, but her power actually followed me. I screamed out in agony when it hit me. I fell to the ground, the pain shooting up my back and into my head. I felt like I was on fire.

I heard the crunch of her footsteps on the gravel driveway. "Poor granddaughter is no match. It saddens me to hurt you this way, but I can't have you getting in my way anymore."

Just as she formed another blue ball, someone came up behind her, snapping her neck.

I glanced up, trying to figure out what was happening. She threatened me one second; the next, she lay on the ground, her head at an odd angle. Was she really dead? I couldn't imagine a snapped neck would kill a goddess.

"It won't kill her, love. That's why we need to get the book and get out of here."

My head snapped up. Lucifer stood before me, wearing another damn suit. "L-Lucifer? Y-You're alive." I could barely get the words out. When I saw something move from the corner of my eye, I pointed. "He's running."

Lucifer chuckled. "Look at him run! Have you ever seen anything like it?" He started to mock him, then stopped and snapped his fingers.

Ashton fell to the ground, screaming, legs bent painfully.

Lucifer walked up to him, hands pushing his suit coat out of the way to rest on his hips. "Ouch. You know, I think that was more how ladies run. Don't you think so, love?" he asked, looking over his shoulder at me.

"I'm not sure what that was. I wouldn't even call that a run, period." I shifted my back, feeling it healing.

Hmm... Interesting.

When I climbed to my feet, I bent over, gritting my teeth. Healing was painful. My skin stitching itself back together. At least that was how it felt. I wanted to curl up into a ball and cry, but I needed to be strong.

I straightened, the pain slowly lessening. When I started to step over Anput to walk toward Lucifer, she grabbed my leg, pulling me down to the ground.

I yelped in surprise, kicking out, hitting her in the face. She cried out, but still managed to move fast enough to get on top of me.

I swung and punched her in the face, blood spurting out of her nose and all over me. I sputtered, but then her hands went around my neck, squeezing. I scrambled to try and pull her hands away.

The lack of oxygen caused my vision to blur. I bucked my body, trying to knock her off. Using maneuvers I remembered from self-defense class, I punched her in the face. When she let go and started to fall to the side, I quickly brought up my leg and kneed her in the head. She grunted as she fell to the ground, but she was quick, scrambling to her feet as I struggled to get to mine. Wasn't it supposed to be easy for me, too?

She kicked out at me, but I stumbled back, barely avoiding it. She started to create another ball of power, but I already held one, throwing it, disintegrating hers.

"How did you do that?" she screeched, then ran at me, hands reaching for my neck again.

I dodged, then swung around her body, grabbed her hair, and pulled. She screamed, flying backward and landing on the ground, hard.

My strength slowly came back. I tried to stomp down on her face, but she rolled, climbing to her feet. I glanced over at Lucifer, seeing him fighting someone. My eyes widened.

The man was huge. Bigger than anyone I had ever seen. What the hell was he? He was slightly deformed, one arm not the same size as the other. I couldn't stop staring.

"What the fuck is that?" I blinked several times, wondering if I imagined it.

When I turned to Anput, I saw her running to the house. I sprinted after her and grabbed her leg just as she made it to the final porch step. She fell and hit her face.

"You bitch!" She kicked out, hitting me in the face.

When I released her, she stood, a smile appearing on her face as another ball formed between her hands. This one seemed to have lightning running through it. The longer she held it, the more power I felt growing.

"I was saving this for later, but I'll use it now. Say goodbye."

I scrambled up as she raised her hand, shifting toward Lucifer and throwing.

I leapt into its path, her power hitting me right in the chest. I screamed, my body bursting into flames. I wanted to roll but couldn't move. I was frozen, the fire consuming me. There was no other pain I could compare it to.

Just as darkness started pulling me under, I felt something radiate in my chest. The light filling me was so bright, I swore I felt its heat.

Slowly, my light consumed the fire, taking it within itself. I felt my strength growing and could now see my surroundings again.

Anput stared down at me, her mouth gaping open. "This cannot be."

I stood, my arms out at my sides. I grinned as I called all the souls to me. I watched the sky light up. As they came closer, they darkened, their true selves revealed. The hope they felt before was gone, causing them to be what they truly were.

The souls filled me, adding to my power. I almost couldn't contain it. It felt cold, like stepping outside after being in a warm house. I directed it toward Anput, my eyes focused on her. I knew they were black, like hers. A sign we were related.

"I should have killed you like I did your mother. Should have killed you both when she was pregnant with you! I was furious when I found out Anubis screwed her."

"You talk too much."

I pushed my hands out in front of me, calling to the souls. They flew from my fingertips. When they hit her body, filling her, she screamed from the pain. There was a burst of bright light, forcing me to shield my eyes with my hand.

When I looked again, she was gone. The souls spun in the air, then flew into the house, toward the book.

I turned to watch Lucifer, his movements still fluid. The giant kept swiping at him. Each time Lucifer threw power at him, it bounced off like a pebble, hitting the ground.

Lucifer kicked him in the chest, causing the giant to stumble back, then he disappeared. The beast looked around, confused. Lucifer reappeared behind the giant and leapt, wrapping his arms around his neck. He grunted, squeezing.

"Come on, you bastard! Give me your fucking head!"

With one hard twist, he tore the giant's head off. As the beast fell to his knees, Lucifer threw the head to the ground and jumped off.

He bent down in front of the head, rubbing at the forehead. When he scratched out some writing, he grinned. "Ah, there we are. Ashton thought he could have this Golem come after me." He kicked the beast's head, then shuddered. "Nasty things."

Seeing my confused look, he pointed at the head. "They write the name of the person controlling it on the forehead. The only way to stop him is to scratch it out. It's hard to accomplish if they're alive. They were going to try and take me out with a Golem!"

He laughed, then opened his arms to me. "Come, love. Give me a hug."

CHAPTER SEVENTEEN

LUCIFER

Feeling my life fading away was probably the scariest thing I'd ever experienced. When you were about to die but couldn't tell anybody, it was a terrible feeling. I knew it was coming. I felt it. At least I spent my last seconds admiring the one I loved. The one who finally came back to me. I couldn't have asked for anything more.

Then Aden woke me and told me to get out of bed. That I had things to do. The shock of coming back to life was tremendous. I was out of breath and too cold to move, almost like someone threw me in ice water. When I saw Aden standing next to the bed, I knew he broke one of his many rules. He wasn't supposed to interfere.

After hearing the story, Maye looked at him. "So, why did you bring him back?" she asked, raising one of her delicate eyebrows. They were too perfect. I had been sitting here, memorizing every feature of her face and body. It was amazing the little things you noticed after cheating death.

Aden looked as if he didn't want to get into it, but when Maye continued to stare at him expectantly, he sighed and shrugged. "He is my brother. I couldn't let someone take him from me. I realized that since a god interfered in the first place, it wasn't *technically* breaking a rule to stop it."

"You didn't want to, though." Anubis shook his head. "He fought with me for hours. I tried talking him into it earlier, but he yelled." He looked at me. "You know how that goes. Nothing is more powerful than Aden's voice."

Snapping my fingers, a cup of tea appeared in my hand. I offered some to Maye, but she only shook her head, focused on Aden. I sipped until it was gone, then threw the cup toward Aden. It disappeared before hitting him.

He pointed at me. "Stop it, Lucifer, or I will send you right back!"

"Is Anput dead?" Maye asked.

Aden shook his head. "No, but she is in a place from where no god can return after breaking the rules. I can't go into details since no one is supposed to know about it." He glanced at Anubis, who held a cup inches from his lips in stunned silence. "Now *he* knows!" Aden threw his hands up. "I must go."

When he disappeared, I looked over at Maye and shook my head. "You've chased him off."

She shrugged. "He was looking for an excuse."

Laughing, knowing she was probably right, I offered her a cup of tea again. She shook her head, now focused on Anubis.

"I'm disappointed in you. You stayed with her, then betrayed her, yet here you are, acting as if nothing happened. I asked you for help and you refused. I'm not sure I can forgive you for that."

The room went silent, Anubis fidgeting nervously. "I do apologize, Maye. I didn't know what to do. Lucifer is a friend, but not my concern. Plus, I knew you could hold your own." He stood, obviously looking for an escape. "I must go find another wife." He waved, disappearing.

I looked over at Maye, who seemed furious that she was left hanging...again. That was what happened with gods.

We didn't care about anybody else. That was how I acted previously, but no more. Not now that Maye was in my life.

I yawned, winking. "Bedtime, love?"

Maye gave me a crooked smile in response. It seemed she was in a good mood after everything. We had gone to Parker's apartment, finding him tied up, yet alive. But the first thing he asked was why she didn't bring the damn painting. I ended up convincing her it was probably for the best that it went into the gallery, yet not be sold.

A few days had passed since everything. Maye now had the book, hiding it somewhere not even I knew about. She put a piece of her own heart next to mine in the book since, according to her, our hearts would never be separated again. It was very sweet, even though I wasn't the sentimental type. I was just happy the souls were confined again, though the world was now confused about what happened. The government's Supernatural Crime Division swept in, telling everyone it was a prank played by local kids. People would probably believe it after a while.

We were back in Hell, my true home. Maye was a little frightened at first because people only heard bad things about Hell. I hoped to keep her from those, but considering there were so many corrupt souls in the world, I didn't think it possible.

Turning to look at her, I realized she was no longer next to me. Confused, I stood to go look for her.

Looking in the bedroom, I saw her standing there, wrapped in my red bathrobe. The color looked amazing against her skin. It reminded me of the fires of Hell. After all, it was my favorite thing. When she dropped the robe, my mouth fell open at the bikini she wore. She then spun around, her ass lighting up with my name in blinking lights. I started laughing, unable to contain myself.

I walked to her and pulled her into my arms, briefly kissing her on the lips. "You are mine now."

"I know. It's pretty much stamped on my ass."

"Yes, and that ass belongs to me. Don't you forget it, love."

"Never."

"Never is right. You're always mine. Always and forever."

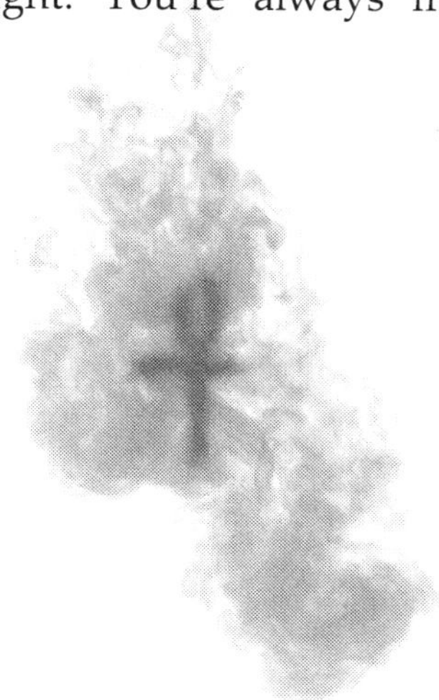

And now a letter from your neighborhood Lucifer…

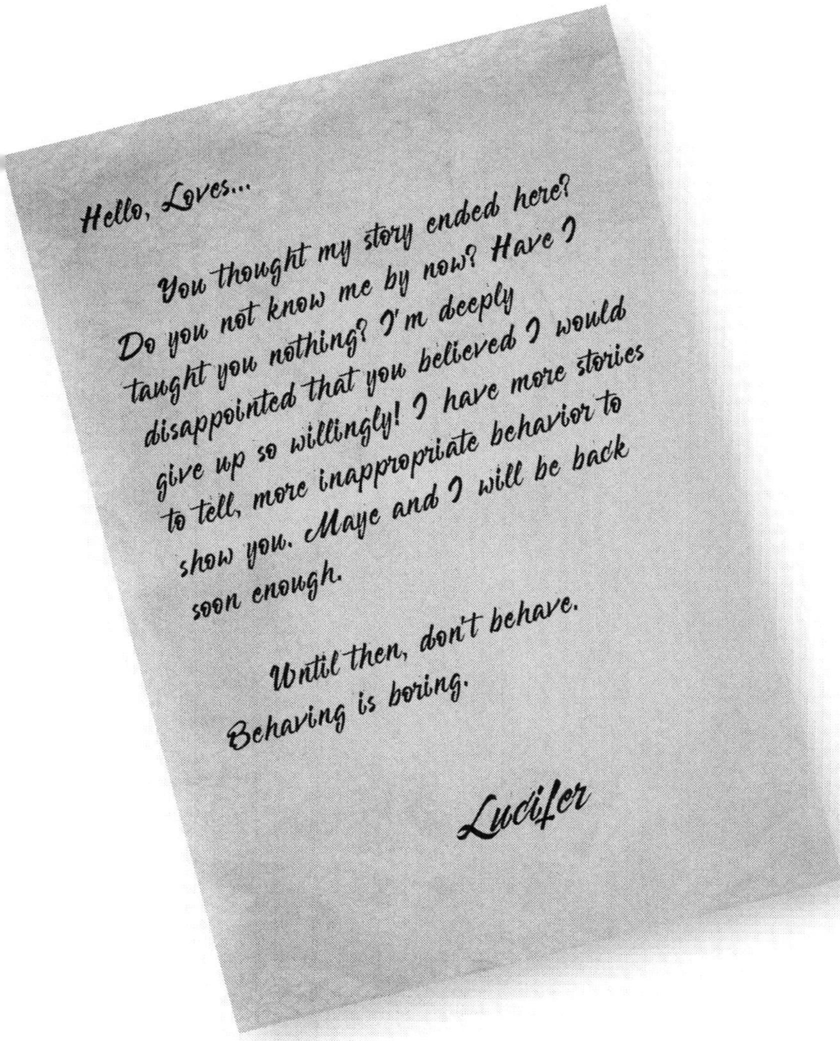

Hello, Loves…

You thought my story ended here? Do you not know me by now? Have I taught you nothing? I'm deeply disappointed that you believed I would give up so willingly! I have more stories to tell, more inappropriate behavior to show you. Maye and I will be back soon enough.

Until then, don't behave. Behaving is boring.

Lucifer

Printed in Great Britain
by Amazon

32768545R00077